Glimmer Train Stories

PUBLISHED QUARTERLY
in spring, summer, fall, and winter by
Glimmer Train Press, Inc.
710 SW Madison Street, Suite 504
Portland, Oregon 97205-2900 U.S.A.
Telephone: 503/221-0836
Facsimile: 503/221-0837
www.glimmertrain.com

PRINTED IN U.S.A.

Glimmer Train (ISSN #1055-7520), registered in U.S. Patent and Trademark Office, is published quarterly, $32 per year in the U.S., by Glimmer Train Press, Inc., Suite 504, 710 SW Madison, Portland, OR 97205. Second-class postage paid at Portland, OR, and additional mailing offices. POSTMASTER: Send address changes to Glimmer Train Press, Inc., Suite 504, 710 SW Madison, Portland, OR 97205.

ISSN # 1055-7520, ISBN # 1-880966-23-9, CPDA BIPAD # 79021

DISTRIBUTION: Bookstores can purchase *Glimmer Train Stories* through these distributors:
Anderson News Co., 6016 Brookvale Ln., #151, Knoxville, TN 37919
Bernhard DeBoer, Inc., 113 E. Centre St., Nutley, NJ 07110
Ingram Periodicals, 1226 Heil Quaker Blvd., LaVergne, TN 37086
IPD, 674 Via de la Valle, #204, Solana Beach, CA 92075
Peribo PTY Ltd., 58 Beaumont Rd., Mt. Kuring-Gai, NSW 2080, AUSTRALIA
Ubiquity, 607 Degraw St., Brooklyn, NY 11217

SUBSCRIPTION SVCS: EBSCO, Faxon, READMORE

Subscription rates: One year, $32 within the U.S. (Visa/MC/check).
Airmail to Canada, $43; outside North America, $54.
Payable by Visa/MC or check for U.S. dollars drawn on a U.S. bank.

Attention short-story writers: *We pay $500 for first publication and onetime anthology rights. Please include a self-addressed, sufficiently stamped envelope with your submission.* ***Send manuscripts in January, April, July, and October.*** *Send a SASE for guidelines, which will include information on our Short-Story Award for New Writers.*

Dedication

We dedicate this issue to Dr. Carl Sagan,
who died on December 20, 1996.

I never said it. Honest. Oh, I said there are maybe 100 billion galaxies and 10 billion trillion stars. It's hard to talk about the Cosmos without using big numbers. I said "billion" many times on the Cosmos *television series, which was seen by a great many people. But I never said "billions and billions." For one thing, it's too imprecise. How many billions are "billions and billions"? A few billion? Twenty billion? A hundred billion? "Billions and billions" is pretty vague. When we reconfigured and updated the series, I checked—and sure enough, I never said it …*

Astonishingly, "billions and billions" stuck. People liked the sound of it. Even today, I'm stopped on the street or on an airplane or at a party and asked, a little shyly, if I wouldn't—just for them—say "billions and billions."

"You know, I didn't actually say it," I tell them.

"It's okay," they reply. "Say it anyway."

—Excerpt from *Billions and Billions*,
by Carl Sagan

On the one hand, it's disconcerting to know he won't be accompanying us into the 21st century.

Photo credit Sam Jones/Montage

On the other hand, we don't believe it one whit.

Susan & Linda

CONTENTS

CONTENTS

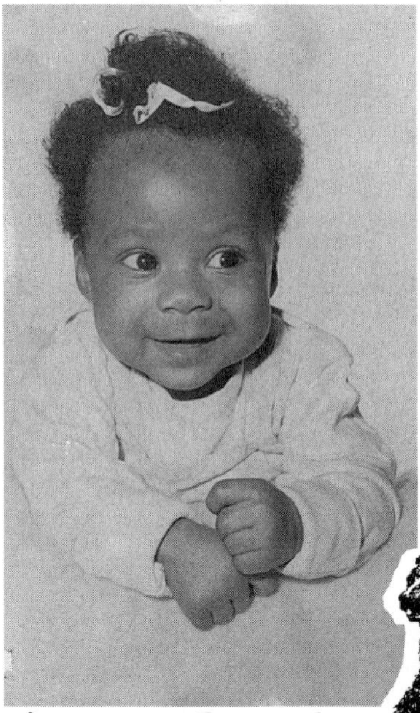

Karen Outen

I was only three months old here. My parents hired a professional photographer, who captured my first on-camera smile.

Karen Outen's short fiction has appeared in *Essence* magazine, *conditions* literary magazine, and the *North American Review*. Over the past five years, she has participated in fiction readings throughout the Philadelphia area. She attended the MFA program in creative writing at Sarah Lawrence College in the early 1980s. Outen has worked in higher education most of her adult life, with a brief stint in corporate communications. She presently works in law-school admissions on programs that promote diversity in legal education.

Although Outen considers the Washington, D.C. area to be home, she lives in Philadelphia, where she was born.

KAREN OUTEN

What's Left Behind

He sweeps by me. My husband, Dizzy, rushes past me with his arms outstretched like a preacher at altar call. He sweeps by nearly on his back. His lower body is invisible beneath the water. I'll never forget his face: raging against this sudden tide. He is stunned to leave me this way. Take my hand, he screams to me. He sweeps by. I will never know if he meant so that I could save him or follow the flow. My family is driftwood floating by: daughter, daughter, husband. I hold tight to the car. I am strapped into the backseat, held in place by the water which rises against my chest. Trying so hard to recount: how did we get here?

Moments ago, in what I see now as a past life: we are in the car. Dizzy drives us home from Keisha's music lesson, Geena's ballet class, a trip to the hardware store. He says: Look at Main Street. It's all crowded. A little rain and folks act too scared to take their known roads. So we take our usual road, an old backroad that is unusually deserted, even considering how small this town is—small and quiet, tucked beneath the mountains which lend a kind of awe and benevolence to our lives. We are insignificant in the world. We know it, and go about our small business easy as you please. We drive pretty slow here. By and large, Sundays are for morning church and afternoon visiting.

Glimmer Train Stories, Issue 24, Fall 1997

This town, Ladyslipper, knows her limits, I believe. No fast food, no high rises. Only 2,000 people live here, half of them driving ten-, fifteen-year-old cars.

So in our old car we take our old road because the rain has stopped finally after four days, and the kids have stopped bugging me to read about Noah's Ark. I sit on the backseat behind Dizzy, as usual. Keisha's up front and Geena's beside me. We bump on the soggy road. The baby inside my womb kicks a swift protest. Then we hear the hard "Bang!" loud and shocking as a cannon, as we lurch forward and down into a deep pothole. We bounce and jerk there a minute. My forehead slams the headrest in front of me and tunnels of pain shoot through my head. My girls scream. I feel sick. Our front tires are stuck so deep that the back tires don't touch the ground. We're rutted midway up the hubcaps.

Goddamn! Dizzy says, It's a wonder we didn't flip! His nose is bloody. He holds his chin. See? See, girls? he says. That's why Mommy and Daddy make you wear seat belts. He reaches for Keisha, who's beside him: You'da gone right through the windshield without that seat belt. Damn. That's the axle gone, I'll bet.

I throw up in my lap, into my maternity pants and thin sweater. I hardly hear them get out of the car, the girls running behind Dizzy, anxious to see a broken axle, whatever that is. My seat belt loose but still buckled, I swing my legs out of the car. Hold tight to the door and put my head near as I can between my knees. My feet swing above the ground.

Look, look, Daddy! The car's off the ground. Wow! The girls run to the back of the car, peer under the tires; it's so unusual to see them off the ground. I remember Dizzy was driving slow over the potholes, fifteen miles an hour. Maybe we'd all be dead now if he'd gone faster.

Dizzy says: Listen. What's that? I listen but my head aches too much to hear anything. I shrug: I don't hear a thing. A few minutes later, still inspecting the back of the car and pinching the bridge of his nose to stop the bleeding, he says it again: What's that roar? Listen. I hold tight to the door to steady myself. I'm still shaken. Look up and catch his eyes, the two grey lashes on his left eyelid, that spidery brown mole in the white of his eye. This look I remember now as a caress.

I hear a roar, and the world explodes. Not a warning drop, but a solid wall of water hits us. The car tilts forward. My legs and crotch get soaked. I hold tight to the car door jam as the water grabs at my legs. The car door slams wide open. Dizzy is screaming to my children. Screaming with the conviction that his voice could be a life raft.

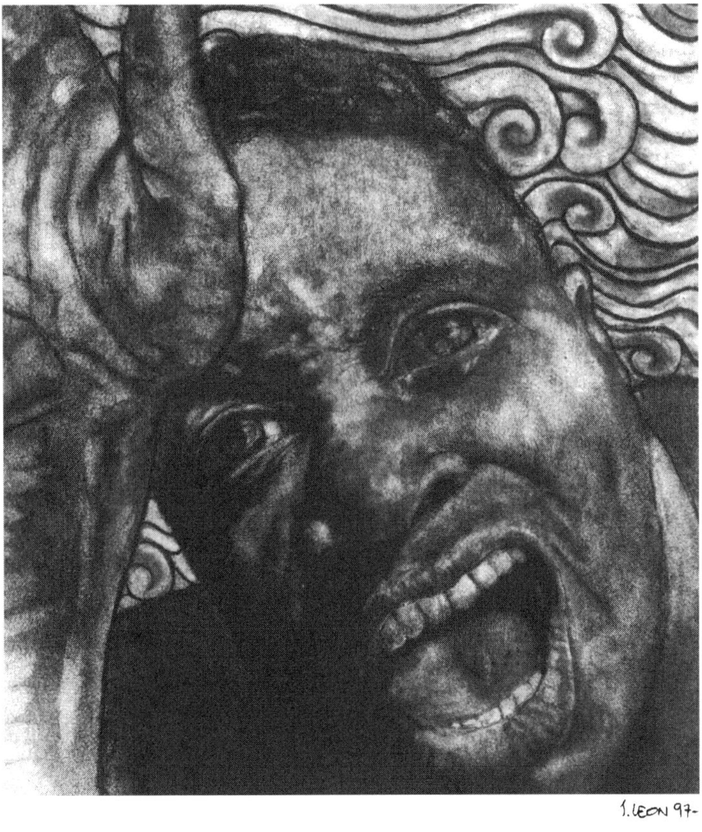

J. LEON 97-

Geena goes first—six years old and tiny, even as an infant too thin for Pampers. She flows off backwards, mouth open wide and speechless. Facing me. Her braids are soaked. Quickly, she's just a head bobbing on the water. I think how hard a time I'll have combing her hair now that it's wet and nappy. Water around my pregnant belly. Grip the inside door handle. My brown knuckles nearly white from strain. Can't remember: can she swim? Was it Geena I took to the Water Babies swim class or Keisha?

Keisha: Dizzy grabs her collar with one hand and the car bumper with the other. Water pulls her away, a great tug-of-war and Keisha's eyes are squinted tight. Dizzy bites his lip and holds on, trembling ... one, two, three ... It goes so slowly, so fast ... four, five, six ... I kick my legs up and fight with the water. I rise, my legs pulled straight out and splayed open ... seven, eight, nine ... She glides to me, arms first. Dizzy grips a purple scrap of her shirt. He holds it fierce as she grabs for me: Hold Mommy's leg. Keisha pulls tight, and I stretch long and rubbery. One hand down to her around my swollen belly. Our eyes lock. She is my determined child. The one who learned to throw herself out of the crib when she did not want to nap. I stare into her eyes. Reaching. The baby in my womb is in the way. I cannot bend, only pull myself lopsided. Come to Mommy, Keisha. The seat belt remains tight. Dizzy put in an extension last month to fit around my high, round belly. Keisha slides. My pantyhose rip. I slap at the water. We hold hold hold our eyes. She slides, grabs my shoe. I grip my toes. But the shoe comes off and she sets sail, whirling away. Holding my shoe, a makeshift steering wheel, she zigzags side to side. And he sweeps by me. Calling me to him. How can I not follow? I hold tight to the door frame. Slammed hard by the water. My legs are sucked beneath the surface. The water rises quickly against my chest. I am still strapped in. The car is rutted deep, the rear of it pushed ever higher by the water. While its joints sigh and moan, the car door hangs open, an unhinged mouth. The baby in my womb closes itself as a fist.

Open my eyes at the hospital. The ambulance stops and out I pour. Cameras pointed at me. I lie still, though I am jostled on the stretcher. Cameras lean over me, hot and bright. I hear them say: This is a good one. Feed it through to the networks. Get the shots of her in the water. An ambulance attendant runs beside my stretcher and tells the doctor about me, about what has happened to me—*what has happened to me. what has. happened. to me.* The doctor looks deep into my face, retrieving my girls, my man. He talks to me but he asks nonsense: Do you know where you are? What's your name? Is there anyone we can call? Are you in any pain? I answer in order. Yes. Mommy. No. Yes. He looks back at the ambulance attendant: Flattened affect. Shock, he nods, and pats my arm.

In high school, before Dizzy, I dated a guy who had been flattened. Run over at a slight diagonal up the center of his body: through the crotch, over his stocky torso and his collarbone, and just missing his head. The school-bus tire left ugly tracks, three serrated rows like a zipper. But he lived, after five months of traction. He came back to school slightly taller, crooked, and very thin. I think of Mose Job like I saw him then: on the blacktop in front of our school, lying there inanimate and sticky with blood. And stunned—why is that? Why aren't we ever prepared? That sometimes it's us.

AMERICA TODAY

Father, 2 Children Drown in Swollen River

Ladyslipper—As a pregnant 31-year-old woman watched in horror, her husband and their two young daughters were swept away as the Mehosehannock River spilled over its banks. The family's car had apparently stalled in the path of the oncoming flood. The woman, identified as Maggie Barnes, was rescued by helicopter an estimated 10 minutes after the accident. Flooding caused widespread property damage over a 15-mile area. The Barneses are the only known fatalities.

Day. Night. Day. Night. I think I am awake continually, but the time flashes so quick between light and dark that I suppose I sleep. It is light and a cluster of nurses stands at my door, huddled close to one another. In the dark, someone holds my hand. Light. A nurse says: Sheriff's here. Can he come in? How 'bout your pastor? Dizzy's aunt? No, no, no. I hear her say later that in my sleep I tremble and gulp like I'm choking. Two old women stand at the head of my bed on either side of me, day and night. They are sentinels in pale blue aprons and white uniforms and old-fashioned nurse's caps, stiff and pointed. They coo to me and stroke my brow. Their skin is the color of mahogany wood and finely textured with lines and spidery veins. I stare at them, picking a new wrinkle or crease to follow each day.

When I dream, I see these women wearing angels' wings. They have come to steal me away to my family. But mostly I dream of Mose on the blacktop. I see rescuers peel him off like PlayDoh. On TV, they show pictures of my empty house, the news people camped out around it. One night I hear the big nurse who cries over me say that they'll release me the next day. So when it is dark and my sentinels doze, I rise and dress quietly. I slip past the nurse at her station, glued to the local TV news and the endless interviews with my children's teachers, my husband's boss. I'm the one you see on TV. *Look-look-look—oh my god, that poor woman.*

THE STATE CAPITOL TIMES

Flooding Hits Home in Ladyslipper

Ladyslipper—Each year scores of Americans are killed in flash floods. But it's never happened here, until now. Since the tragic drowning of Keisha Barnes, 8, her sister Geena, 6, and their father Dizzy, the town of Ladyslipper has grieved openly for the first children it has lost in eight years. Tucked west of a range of mountains known simply as Bobb's, this sheltered hamlet is working class and close knit with a nearly equal number of black and white residents. Their grief for the Barnes family, who was black, crosses racial and gender lines—"Tragedy ain't just doled out according to skin color," Delilah Pyles admonishes a reporter.

"It's a shock," says Norma McInierney. "Feel just like somebody hit me. Everybody knows them. My husband was Dizzy's high-school coach. The thing is, a warm night like this, those little girls would be playing jump rope in my yard right now." She shakes her head, "I can just see 'em."

"Those are my goddaughters and my best friend," says Sheriff Jonah Kind in a halting voice. "I don't know what to do. I keep going by the house to see if it's not some mistake. Some awful mistake."

Mose answers his door. His face holds a terrified calm. The nurses looked at me frightened, too, as if I were contagious.

Good damn, he says, then shakes his head: Oh, Maggie, Maggie. He holds back awhile, then pulls me to him. We rock back and forth, a pitiful box step. Mose never could dance. You're all over the TV, he says when we part.

I nod: I know. Can't go home. Saw them waiting there.

Inside his house, I dangle on a rope inside his TV. Snatched from the water. I remember the rope around my chest. The rubber-padded man, life vest, helmet. I rose heavy. I look away as my TV self parts the water. I collapse on Mose's couch and sigh.

He sits next to me.

There's nowhere else to go, I say.

I know it, he answers.

This is awkward, or rather it should seem more awkward. I have not really talked to Mose for years and years. But I don't feel it, really. I don't feel much at all.

On TV, a fat woman in her twenties with a Life's A Beach T-shirt takes up the screen: I got two babies of my own. I'm from right here in Ladyslipper. You'da had to shoot me if this was to happen to me. I couldn't take it. I couldn't take it, she wails. She scoops up her toddler, hugs his cheek to her mouth, startling the baby until he cries.

Mose takes my hand. And oddly, I am comforted by his scaly skin, by his dusty smell and the smell of his house, which seems to have been closed tight for years. Old newspapers stand along the walls in dozens of neat, tied stacks. Cardboard boxes with lids are topped with glass or plywood for tables.

Haven't had company, he says, and I know he means forever. And I think about him coming back to school, finally, after his accident. With a cane in his hand and his father at his side—his father who was the oldest man in town, nearly eighty-three when Mose was seventeen, and called Mose by his whole name from birth: Mose Job! Mose Job! Come to supper. Mose Job! Pull my car around front. Mose limped into school. Half of us were silent and scared. The rest of us giggled nervously. His skin seemed taut, and he really was taller. All his pants were highwaters. He walked down that long hallway, and we stood in rows by the lockers, all of us: black and white, underclassmen and seniors, staring like a hearse passed us. Staring at Mose Job and his ancient father. They looked alike for the first time. His father had been set apart by his crooked body—even his fingers bent, with the tips jutting forward. But that day Mose Job and his father both leaned forward on canes like sick, tired trees; they matched. A cold dead air fanned behind them as they passed. Until somebody said: Gumby's back! And we laughed so that the air we expelled pumped into Mose's lungs, heated up that deadly pall around him. Until he laughed, too, then waved his long fingers. We brought him back to us—laugh-two-three, laugh—c'mon back, Mose Job.

Mose is sitting beside me when I wake up. I look long and hard at his face. His lips are full and smooth, his thick eyelids darker than his skin so that they seem shaded. It's an expressive face, full of tenderness and sorrow. I study him. I am sorry I never loved him fully. I feel great sadness at that, something desperate and shameful.

He makes me mush and corned-beef hash and biscuits. Only ever cooked for my pops, he says. He ain't have no teeth left.

I eat it. Because what do I care about taste? And, truth be told, it's not bad. But then I notice it for sure. That it's wet in my seat. Not sopping, but wet. While Mose clears the table, I reach inside my panties. A steady trickle of clear liquid seeps out of me. Fishy liquid. It's not my baby's water breaking—no. Something else.

Mose, I say, I need to go in town. To the drugstore.

We walk down the gravel path leading to Peggy's Neck Road. This path, now muddy and calf-high full of water, is the only place I've glimpsed him since I married and had babies. Sometimes driving by I'll see a skinny man darting through the trees, a hand rising through the branches to wave. I know he's lived here alone since his papa died, and he works at the factory in Slippery, next town over. I remember suddenly, startlingly, being here with him one night fourteen years ago back when we were best friends, and more. Here in his field, I took off my panties, rolled my white knee socks down to my ankles, and pushed my blue plaid skirt above my hips. On a blanket, I sat spread-eagle around him, impatient for him. We were eager to become lovers, but doomed: we took useless turns kneading his crushed penis, and we both fought tears. How angry I was with him.

We cut into town mostly through farmland and people's backyards since the main road, Route 78, is flooded. We walk slow and with purpose. But we can't take shortcuts on the side streets because of the police barricades. And the noise, the noise:

the car horns, the hideous rush of water—

Stop walking; I grab Mose's arm. I hear Dizzy say: Listen? What's that roar?

We stand on Side Street in front of Jo-Ellena Fabrics, a two-story whitewashed store that used to be the Pentecostal Church. A woman touches me. Clutches my arm. Praying loud. Another one gasps and runs by me to her husband, who stands at his car. She falls into his arms, crying like a baby. I do not recognize Ladyslipper. There's a new attraction: a natural disaster. Main Street, which ought to spread itself out wide two blocks ahead, seems gone. I can't see the Woolworth's, the Baylor's Drug, the Miss June's Ice Cream tucked neatly beside it, or the three-story, fully stocked Kiddie Town on the corner.

We can't cross to Main. Ahead of us, a river rushes down Gulph Street, which is a perfect riverbed. It's a wide street that dips deep in the middle. Police guard it, pushing people back from the brink of the water—all of our police are here, regulars and auxiliary. Even kids from the high-school police club are here, dressed in dark blue shirts and ties and tan pants, and police caps that sometimes swim on their heads. They look solemn and say softly: Please keep back, ma'am. Townspeople stand against the yellow wooden police barricades and dip their hands in the water. Or throw in flowers. I see small placards and big, gaudy funeral flower arrangements: a broken circle, a teddy bear with huge, tiger-lily eyes. All have this message: God bless you, Keisha and Geena. Nobody mentions Dizzy. Women weep over the water. They wear cotton flowered housedresses or dark knit stretch pants. They share the same face, black or white, old or young, the same look of Ladyslipper: loose, fleshy, like well-worked bread dough. They dimple and crease, slide in and out of sorrow. The women lean on the barricades and sob. They throw not only roses and baby's breath into the water, but kiddie bookbags, hair barrettes and bows, Legos, Barbie dolls, baby dolls. And us. Us.

There are pictures everywhere: Keisha and Geena on lapel pins. On black-and-white posters in store windows. On flyers that say, Pray for our girls, Ladyslipper. Or, Remember Keisha and Geena. Drive with care. *They have been in my house, in my things.* I cry out, and they see me. They reach for me, pulling at the hem of my tunic. Grabbing at my arms. Mose holds me. Thin Mose. They seem to reach through him. We look at each other in sorrow. Helpless. I pray for those girls, someone yells. God bless you. Be strong! My sleeve rips as once more I am engulfed. The Lord is my shepherd, I shall not want. Suffer the little children unto me.

A woman I don't recognize steps forward swiftly and slaps me hard twice: You bitch! You could've saved them!

I sink back into Mose. She is snatched by people on either side of her. They pull and jostle her, swear at her. Mose and I push out of the crowd. My nose bleeds where she hit me. The police scramble, unprepared. Ladyslipper has had one mugging and three robberies in five years. Never an angry crowd.

Water leaks between my legs in stingy drops. It smells like this makeshift river: angry, briny. The clouds hang low and soiled grey, rising just off Bobb's Mountain to the east. I won't get to see Main Street, Miss Hannah's Studebaker parked below her sign: Hannah's Good Eats. Instead, helicopters circle Gulph Street's river, newscopters that trouble the water with their whirly-burly. My children flow by. First, Geena, her braids a thick raft. Then Keisha, steering by my shoe. And Dizzy, sweet Dizzy, calling my name. I am sane now for one reason: I did not see them go under. Only sweep away wild and sudden, his arms open to me, their tiny girlish heads bobbing above water.

THE TIMES OF LADYSLIPPER

Local Landmark Destroyed

Miss Hannah's 1957 Studebaker was destroyed last night in a collision between two news vans. Vans were racing to Gulph Street where Maggie Barnes was spotted, sparking an uprising among the crowd. Miss Hannah's mint-condition Studebaker has been parked outside the diner since her husband, the late Jenkins Jones, drove it here from the factory in Detroit. As in most of northern Ladyslipper, the diner and car had been spared from flooding.

"It was my daddy's dream to own a car, not just a hauling truck. He was so proud when he come home with it," said Lloyd Jenkins Jones this morning.

Miss Hannah was too distraught for comment.

Mose was some kind of celebrity as Gumby. The newspapers wrote story after story on his progress. No other kid in the state had survived being run over by a bus. In the hallways at school or in town, it was: Hey, Gumby Man, what's happening? I tutored him in English so I was one of the few who knew how changed he was. Something about a damaged optic nerve. He could barely see out of his left eye. And I knew he lost his balance a lot. Sometimes he just fell over for no reason. But when he was Gumby, he had this status he hadn't had before the accident. He had been just this shy, average-looking guy who always wore dusty brown penny loafers and corduroys. But not quite a nerd, because he could set a whole class to laugh with his deadpan humor and blank face. He could joke a teacher out of giving the class detention. Nobody even teased him much about his ancient daddy, even though they could have: Mose Job could never much fight. But as I say, as Gumby, everybody wanted to take a picture with Mose, or invite him to their parties. Or court him. Shy Mose—there he is, at the Superfly party in his flannel shirt with the white T-shirt peeking through. He's standing against the wall, smiling shyly at our polyester double knits and wide lapels. He'd stumble out at some respectably late hour and everybody'd joke that he was so quiet in the corner: Must've been getting high, Cool Mose. So I'd go behind him, lead him by the arm. He'd told me that the strobe lights in these dark cinderblock basements made him nightblind. After awhile, he'd just linger near a door 'til I came for him. I'd walk him through the tall alfalfa grass near his home and let him kiss me in the dark. Cold sloppy kisses, nearly swallowing my bottom lip. I was never excited so much as patient and glad. Glad he had somebody to kiss in the dark. I remember his wet, sorry kisses and the breeze in the grass, the way the lower mountains cut a jagged line across the sky. I had some feeling for Mose. Not love. Not pity. Some feeling.

THE HERALD TIMES MAGAZINE

A Flood Runs Through It

Ladyslipper—This is normally an ordinary town of winding back roads and farmland. Today, however, a visitor finds those roads transformed into canals, into a stark set from a futuristic science-fiction movie where dogs paddle by languidly, followed by small chairs and particle-board tables, stuffed bunny rabbits, an occasional dead bird. And where old women gather at the graveyard.

Miss Janice Hoover, 70, the former principal of the Colored Normal School, helps her 89-year-old mother navigate the flood waters. They have visited the grave of Miss Janice's father every day for 23 years. This day will not be an exception. The Hoovers occasionally identify the belongings they pass—"Miss Norrisson's side chair," "Mr. Waples' cane stand"—as they wade in thigh-high water that is cold and nearly still.

At the end of New Deal Street, they reach a plot where the brown water is filled with muddy, half-submerged headstones. Two police deputies sit on the hood of a stalled car, and old women—black and white—are camped out on either side of them. Some sit in the high cabs of pickup trucks with oversize tires. Others sit atop the hoods of stranded cars and recline against the windshields. Some knit, some read from their Bibles, others just "keep company." As the Hoover women approach, the

> deputies help them climb aboard.
>
> "So many of our porches done flooded or collapsed," says Sudie Nickels, 81. "We don't have no place to gather. Plus, it's sort of keeping watch on our children, those babies and their father what was lost. It's our way to sit a vigil at the wake, and since we got no bodies, we've got to do it this way. I was their great grandmother's best friend, you know, God rest her soul."

I lay on Mose's couch. It's nighttime and the dusty windows absorb the darkness ... Next, I am leaning over the creek behind the house, my face inches from the water, my nose touching it. Mose lifts my shoulders, wipes my face, guides me back to his house. It is so dark. I am confused and I long for moonlight. Mose, Mose, I call. Yep, he answers soft.

Again, I must recount: how did I get here? I was on the couch, still soggy and soft between my legs. I concentrated on Mose's house, which smells like Ben Gay and old newspapers. I thought: I can't sleep here. But I suppose I did.

Back in his house, Mose sits me in a hardback chair and peels the nightshirt from me. He washes my feet and legs, slow, gentle rubbing. My hands smell surprisingly of fish. We both look at them with anger.

Mose went from being Gumby to Mose Job the Fish on a class trip to SeaLand. There we stood in a dimly lit room full of fish swimming behind glass walls. Who saw it first? The blue fish with striped gills, its back arched like a football. And flat as your hand. So odd surrounded by fat fish who swam faster. Who said it? "Look. Look, y'all, it's Mose Job." Flat and blue laying there on the blacktop: CPR, electric shock—how do we get this boy to breathe again? "Look, y'all, Mose the Fish." He looked at it, such a sad startled look. He shuddered. We nudged him: "Say something." But Mose and this fish were locked in, somehow. "Say something clever, Mose Job." He touched the glass and pulled his hand away quick and walked away. Walked out of our lives.

I sob suddenly into my hands. My fishy hands. He takes them, too, soaks them in lemon juice and a little ammonia, then dresses me in a fresh nightshirt. I look down at its old threads, weak and soft.

Papa's, he says.

He makes up the couch again, straightens my sheets, fluffs my pillows which ooze their stuffing white and silky; they are lost clouds come to make my bed. He stands holding the blanket to put over me. I think of his sweet, messy kisses and shake my head. He mimics me, confused. I point to his bedroom. He drops the blanket and sinks down on the couch.

Not a good plan, he says weakly.

Maybe ten minutes, maybe half an hour, we sit. Nothing happens or moves, except the smell of this house seeps into me. Already there's a layer of dust or sediment that seems to coat my lungs. Sometimes I cough to see what rises from my alluvial soil. Finally he gets up. I feel him before I see him. Leaning over me. He takes my hand and leads me to his bed. Feels like a pile of three or four old mattresses. We sink in and cover ourselves with moth-eaten wool blankets, their satin edges frayed.

He takes my hand and strokes it, wonderful, like these are his first fingers, the first flesh he has known. I kiss him. He lifts my hand and places it on his side: See, he says. Used to be my spleen. Gone.

He moves my hand down to his groin. Moves my fingers under his penis, which is moist, prickly, and cool. Our fingers grope his empty sac.

They're retracted. Pushed inside I don't know where. Maybe where my kidney used to be. Ain't nothing like it was.

My fingers swim in his empty space. I move them over the wide vein of his penis, up to his soft patch of hair. Baby's hair, curly, thick, and strong. I brush my cheek against his shoulder. The skin is scarred where it was grafted. Also, dry and ashy. I sigh and the moist air I exhale softens his skin, makes it tender and almost for a moment like he's fifteen years old again. But he is right. Nothing's as it was. I hold the base of his penis, this delicate, wilted flower.

Later, Mose takes my hand and pulls me from the bed. He helps me put on shoes and an old flannel work shirt over the nightgown. There is still no moonlight as we walk. We step high in the tall grass. Mud oozes into my shoes and chills me. Mose holds my hand so tight. We walk a mile, grass whisking against us—shushh, shushh. The slender grass feels like tiny hands across my thighs, my baby, my arms; it brushes against me and I feel comforted. The blades of grass are small and yielding as babies' hands, old women's hands, patting me, soothing me—shush, shushhh, shushh—my baby folds itself in prayer—shush, shushhh—we find solace, as if all of Ladyslipper hides in this grass, comes to guide me—shush, shushh—it is my people, my Ladyslipper I find here. The tall grass moans and bends to my aid.

Beyond us, the river looms closer as we walk. Closer, louder. I pull back once, but Mose comes for me, his arms around my shoulders; he pushes me on. Eerie now, my comfort gone. The river swallows and gulps. I think of the nurse who said I gulped in my sleep. A stench overtakes Ladyslipper, so strong and sour that my eyes burn. We cross the parking lot for the new Baptist Church, the majority of which has peeled away and slid down into the river. The remainder of the church sits sliced clean open, its pews and altar bowing down toward the water. Mose stops walking. I turn to him.

It's a comfort, he says: That it couldn't happen again. You'll see.

He folds his body down, sinks onto the cracked pavement, and stretches full out, arms to the sides, legs apart, head turned hard to the left. So hard that his face presses into the pavement; hard enough to smell the school bus tires: rubber, sulfur, and traces of manure from the country roads. He closes his eyes.

I walk toward the stagnant water. Glance back at Mose, who watches me now. Straight on to the flow. I feel a deep terror. I stop. I step gingerly to a large rock. A skinny but sturdy tree grows behind it and drapes down over the water. Fearful, then defiant and unflinching, I struggle for balance on the rock—I see myself plunge backwards into this open wound of a river, I sink then rise in a long purple robe, belted in gold threads; yes, that was me, twelve years old and baptized here, flung in a sinner and retrieved in salvation. My mother and father were still alive then, and they wept on the shores as I rose, whole and new.

I waddle on this solid rock, squat my knees for balance, and latch onto the tree. Nervous, I sweat and feel chilled. Excited, I am light-headed and mocking disaster. Hold tight and stretch out, wrap my bare arms around this splintery tree trunk. Water floods my shoes, pulls at my legs, swipes at me furious. I feel a sinking fear but I see: I am safe. I cannot be had this time—*this time!* What washes over me is a strange relief. A sudden shame. It is done, and still … I survive.

Mose has been answering the phone a lot this morning. Outside there's a ruckus. He says: They found us.

I sit down at the kitchen table, which is piled high with cakes, pies, a glazed ham, a homemade loaf of wheat bread, some kind of noodle casserole. Found 'em on the steps, he says: Folks are kind.

The phone rings. Mose talks briefly and then comes to the table. We sit facing each other. Sipping strong coffee in our nightshirts. Perfectly quiet. Perfectly removed. There's a sort of comfort and woe I cannot describe. Shut up in this house. Listening to the crunch of tires on gravel. Heavy-handed knocking on the doors. We're sealed tight behind dingy grey windows. So little light in here. I wipe my hand across the kitchen table. Looks to have a thick coat of grey dust, but nothing wipes off on my hand. Should we let people in? I look around. The couch still holds my bedding, the armchair's leg is broken and it leans heavy to the right. What passes for an ottoman is really just a stack of tied magazines with a scarf thrown over it. I won't let anyone in. They wouldn't understand this home ... home. Mine has Beauty and the Beast and Little Mermaid, Princess Jasmine, a harem of Barbie dolls, hair barrettes and ribbons hidden all over the house like Easter eggs.

He answers the phone. Pitifully thin Mose standing sideways and bent, patting his foot, nervous. He turns to me: You should take this one. It's not the talk-show people. It's Jonah Kind.

He holds the phone up to my ear. I clutch the coffee cup in one hand, rub my neck with the other.

Maggie? Maggie? Jesus— I didn't know where you were. Are you all right? Oh, Maggie ... Listen, I'm sorry to have to ask this, but I'm gonna have to ask you to come into the station. We need some kind of formal record of the accident. It's just my job. Maggie, I apologize, Jonah mumbles into the phone.

I move my head away from the receiver. Mose says to Jonah: Fine, but all these news folk are here. How we gonna get out?

I'll come for you then, Jonah tells him, and it booms out of the phone.

I wonder what he does now at night, I say.

Who?

Jonah. He used to come by every night. Walk in and go straight to the refrigerator like he was home. Or go tuck in the girls when Dizzy worked late. Listen to my stories about my day. Mose?

Yeah?

What d'you suppose he does at night now?

Mose blinks fast, then turns away.

I get dressed to go to the police station. Dressed in the same thin sweater and soiled maternity pants I wore That Day. But my clothes are clean. Mose has washed them by hand, scrubbing them with even strokes on an old washboard. I watched him, though he didn't see me—watched how gingerly he touched the polyester silk of my bra and the cotton of my sweater, how he clutched them to his face a long time. I wear Mose Job's daddy's boxer shorts for underpants and I still drip-drip my water. I am never quite dry. I come into the kitchen. Mose slices ham, shoves thick slabs between wheat bread, heaps collard greens and kale onto paper plates. One by one he passes them out the living-room window. Thanks, they say. Much obliged. The window's open just enough to fit hands and paper platters through it. It brings a slender ribbon of light to cut across the room, a sudden brightness that I can't bear. I rest flat against the wall, which is easy because despite my high, full belly, I grow thinner, my arms and legs and face less fleshy, my back feeling bony. What will this new baby think of me, of this thin, quiet mother, a sort of cut-out doll? Flat. And moist: how old will I grow and still leak what has seeped into me? I look behind me for the trail I surely make. I could leave watery figure-eight's like graffiti as I grow old and copper skinned, dancing through Main Street of an evening.

I watch Mose—never saw him move so fast, small beads of sweat on his forehead. Purpose feeding him, pumping into his skinny veins, his hollowed cheeks. Mose Job nearly smiles.

A man's hand pushes back a plate of food. He says: It's Jonah Kind, Mose. Can I come 'round?

Sheriff Jonah Kind pushes his way past reporters and townsfolk—some of them Dizzy's distant kin, I see—and angles his way through the door. He takes stock of the room a long time. Mose stands, hands folded obediently in front of him. Jonah Kind scans the room slow, mesmerized, adjusting to the near-light of my makeshift home. It's clear he doesn't see me. I cough.

Maggie? That you?

Yeah, Jonah. It's me.

Whew, he says, and comes over in big steps like he's wading

against tide. He's the biggest-chested man I know. He steps in front of me. I watch his chest rise and fall. He sighs heavy and takes me into his arms. God, Maggie, he says over and over. I loved him. I loved him.

Heah, Jonah, how 'bout a cup of coffee? Folks dropped some off this morning, Mose says.

Jonah releases me. Mose walks toward the kitchen and I hear him mumble, incredulous: Cup of coffee? Sit awhile for some coffee? He repeats it, testing out inflections.

Nah, Jonah says. His skin is about Dizzy's color and texture. I look away from him. Got my deputies outside, to help y'all get to the station. Ready?

Jonah Kind belongs to Ladyslipper. When he was four years old, Felbo Toussand found Jonah in his fields, curled up beside a milking cow, asleep on her teats. He was half-frozen and scrawny. Felbo and his wife wrapped Jonah in warm blankets, took moist towels and liniment to his raw feet, fed him lentil soup and biscuits. They held him in their arms constantly because he shivered so, even after he was warmed. For weeks he shivered and cried, and the Toussands held him. Later, he stammered as though his teeth still chattered. So all winter, on an old loveseat in front of the fireplace, Felbo and Minnie Toussand held Jonah nestled between them until he settled there and took root.

Nobody ever got the straight story on where he came from. They just took him in. Everybody—Felbo for the first two years 'til his wife died, then the Hendricks, the Norrissons, the Nickels, the Hoovers, even my family, all took a turn, depending on who could afford an extra mouth that year. Not like shuffling him, more like he was a new baby at a family reunion, passed from warm arms to warm arms, cradled and cooed over. He even stayed with a couple white families in high school so he could get to the demonstration school in Slippery. He lived with Dizzy's family awhile, and he and Dizzy became best friends for life. When he graduated with honors from high school, the town council paid his way to state college. He's every kid's Uncle Jonah, everybody's brother or son. When he was sworn in as Sheriff and the judge asked his parents to stand, every man and woman over fifty stood up. But the drawback is, he says, every woman in town feels like a relative, so he doesn't date.

I sit between Jonah Kind and Mose Job in the back of the squad car. Jonah takes my hand in his, turns it over and over slowly, like a marble.

Outside the room, people clamor for us. We sit at a long pine table. When I run my hand across it, I remember its story. I get up and walk around it, looking under the sides, feeling my way. Mose frowns at me.

Oh! Jonah gasps and springs up so fast he rocks the table: Here it is.

I walk around to the far right side of the table, near the back corner of the room. Jonah runs his finger along the wood grain, then lifts the table up so I can see it. Scratched there in immature scrawl: First, Butch and Sundance. Now, Jonah and Dizzy.

I've never seen this before, I say, and smile: Skipping school in fifth grade. You two were a couple of rebels. Without a clue. I laugh and I can see Dizzy's silly smirk and hear his reply: Ha ha ha, Miss Honor Roll. Jonah puts the table down. He kneels in front of it and rests his forehead against it. He makes no noise as he cries. I walk back across the room to leave him in peace. I stare through the glass wall. They cannot see me through the blinds, but I count twenty men and women with microphones and notepads and tape recorders.

What for? I ask aloud.

Mose comes to me. For you, he says: For your story.

Jonah rises, sniffing. Jonah Kind is the softest-hearted man I know, Dizzy used to tell me. Jonah sits heavy in front of me, and says: I shouldn't be the one to do this. You and Dizzy are my family. I can't interrogate you.

I laugh and reach for his hand: Hell, Jonah, we're all your family. He smiles and I pull my hand away quick because I feel his sorrow pulling for me.

What d'ya need to know? Mose asks.

What happened that day. Maggie, you remember?

I shrug: Sure. Every day.

So I tell him everything, just as I went over it in my head all that time I was strapped in that damned car, the cold water up to my collarbone and smacking toward my ears. Mose stands stock still while I talk. Jonah holds his chin and shakes his head, his eyes bloody wet.

I say: Nothing was unusual. No premonitions. Nothing. Keisha and Geena did their usual. Geena likes to tattletale that Keisha won't brush her teeth. Every morning she comes downstairs and says to me, Smell her breath, then points to her sister—

My words just stop. Just shut off like a faucet. I stare clear eyed and silenced.

Well, Jonah stutters: I s-s-s-up-pose I c-can write up a re- re— He pulls a piece of twine from his shirt pocket and works it with both hands, slow and methodical. He clears his throat. Just need some kind of accident report on file, he says slowly.

We'll never find the bodies, will we? I ask.

Jonah stiffens and his fair skin seems to drain more of its color before he turns ruddy. No, he answers: They're saying with that part of flooding emptying into the Atlantic it could be months. Or never. They're gone, Maggie.

No, no, I know, Jonah. I understand.

A deputy at the door says the media wants a statement, they know I'm in here. Jonah pushes him away and closes the door. I sit at the long table, my hands folded in front of me. Mose stands to my left, his corduroy pants baggy in the hips. I can nearly see his pelvic bone protrude. Jonah blocks the door. You don't have to, Maggie, he says, soft but stern: You don't have to talk to them a bit.

I nod: Hadn't planned to.

Okay, he says: Now, tell me what you'd like for me to say. I'll take care of it.

Mose walks to the glass wall, hands shoved hard in his pockets. He peers out, half-blind Mose. I watch him awhile. He turns to me slowly. I'll go, he says.

Jonah looks up at him: Say what?

Well, Mose begins slowly: You're the sheriff. You gotta represent the town. I can speak on behalf of Maggie.

Jonah frowns: I don't see where Maggie and Ladyslipper have competing interests. You forget, maybe nobody else lost like this, but Felbo lost all his milk cows, Miss Ethel and Miss Mae's whole front porch and parlor broke off and washed away. The Yules' lost everything in that little house, all their belongings just washed out the front door. Everybody lost something even if it was just a house, not a friend or a husband or children.

So you talk on the town. I'll talk on Maggie.

Now, s-s-see here, Jonah raises his voice and taps on the table.

No, I say: Mose is right. He can talk for me. That'll be fine.

Jonah glares at me, that glare at my insubordination just like Dizzy. But I keep focused on Mose, who nods slowly and drinks me in. Mose Job.

Well, so what do you want him to say?

He knows.

Reads minds, does he?

I take Jonah's hand. He remains testy, and when I look at him he seems deeply hurt. It's no offense, I say softly, then I kiss his hand, which is fat with stubby fingers and dark, hairy knuckles. He sighs: All right, Maggie. Immediately I feel guilty. This is how I coaxed Dizzy—was it this generic, that it could've been any man? I look at Mose. He stares with longing outside the room.

I can hear them fine once they go out. Mose recounts the story of the flood, nearly word for word as I hear it in my mind. Mose Job looks at ease at the podium. He talks slow and even and forceful. His shoulders set back and his chin juts forward. It looks like a dance, the reporters alternately scribbling on their pads and popping up their arms for questions, Mose pointing to recognize one or the other, this back and forth that he does with ease and skill and grace. And I swear, each wave of his arm, each gesture to recognize puts a glow on his face. He grows larger in their spotlight. And I see us all as teenagers, lining those high-school hallways watching him return to us: C'mon back, Mose Job.

When he's finished, he comes back to me and takes my hand. He holds it light but sure, as fragile as I hold him.

Jonah watches us, unable to decode our language. I didn't know you two were so close, he says.

I think now of Dizzy—his touch, the sex of his sigh, the anticipation and pleasure of his skin on mine, the steady undertow that swept me to him. I close my eyes and concentrate on Mose's scaly, dry hand. There is something flat and desperate between us.

Jonah looks at me, guarding Dizzy. I go to him. Please don't judge me, I say.

He exhales and his bulky arm wraps around me, pulls me tight to him. He says: Maggie, d'you know what I miss? Watching you put our girls to bed. Hearing you sing to them. He whispers: It's the only thing that reminds me of my mother. It's like, you carry that for me.

I sink into his arms, into what is familiar. Here, in Jonah's arms, he still cradles my babies, he hugs Dizzy, and lifts and twirls me on my wedding day—the scenes of my life spill from his opened arms, his familiar scent of backyard barbecues and spring tulips planted under my windows; this tender place, this home—even now if I close my eyes, he is my high four-poster bed, the basket of sneakers by the back door, all jumbled sizes and colors nestled there—this place ... this, this is all that is left of me ... but I fear it. It is not real. I pull away. I reach for Mose's hand quietly, one hand behind my back toward him. I latch on.

THE HERALD TIMES

As River Recedes, Normalcy Remains Elusive

Ladyslipper—Sheriff Jonah Kind is ubiquitous. As flood waters recede, he's become a busy man. During the day, he can be found shoveling the brown sludge out of the homes of the town's elderly. Or talking to Felbo Toussand about his plans to replace his drowned livestock. Each day he speaks to schoolchildren about the dangers of playing in flood waters. But by night he ignores his own admonitions. He wades through the flood waters or travels the more treacherous river by boat, with a rope and netting by his side and a spotlight in hand. He drags the river, searching for the body of Dizzy Barnes, the best friend to whom he occasionally refers as his brother. Sheriff Kind figures that while the bodies of Barnes' daughters may have been swept far from town, Barnes may still be found near here.

"He's a big guy like me. Couldn't swim so hot. I figure, maybe he just sank or got stuck on a tree trunk. Maybe it's illogic," he shrugs. "I don't know what else to do."

At home tonight, after we come from our places—his blacktop, my river—I dress for bed. Mose squirrels up in a corner of the living room. He pores over his scrapbook:

Boy Run Over By School Bus, Survives.

Crushed Boy In Critical Condition.

Boy, Flattened By Bus, Returns To School.

He reads each article slowly, runs his hands over the photos of him in traction, of him returning to school with his cane, of Mose and his daddy.

In this deep cottony crater that serves as our bed, Mose crawls to me and embraces my belly. I reach for him, tracing his scars with trembling fingers. I ply my fingers through his moist hair, push aside his penis, and reach for the loose, soft sac. I touch him and it is almost myself I touch. I grow expectant and tender. He lays still. Awkwardly, I move myself down in the bed inching to him on elbows until my face meets his groin. It is warm and musty there as a basement, a locked attic. I kiss him tenderly. I kiss what is empty, loving this forsaken space. His skin is salty and sweet. I hold and caress and kiss him. Mose strokes my hair and sobs: It's been so long.

I know, I say.

I wake up late, after noon. I hear voices coming from the living room. When I emerge, the window is open wide and Mose stands talking with reporters and the neighbors. The kitchen has become practically a restaurant. He takes orders, makes plates heaping with food, tells jokes, asks: Another cup of coffee?

Jonah Kind is sitting at the kitchen table sipping coffee. He flips through Mose's pile of junk mail, and he looks like he's been here everyday of his life. He looks up at me and smiles: Mose here makes a mean cup of coffee. Can I pour you some?

The room's normal grey is offset by long streams of sunlight that cut a translucent yellow band around the room. It seems to swirl. The people at the window call to me, pointing cameras in. Their hands reach in and wave, grab at me—*take my hand!*—I rush to the window, snatch it down, nearly crushing hands, leaving long, cleaned-off streaks on the glass. My fingers cake with the sludge of moistened dust. I see their bobbing heads and troubled faces through the cleaned streaks.

What's wrong with you people? I yell. Mose and Jonah are stock still: What is this? What is this?

Just being hospitable, Maggie, Mose says. He holds two plates piled so high with food that the plate bottoms sag and soak up grease. His biceps bulge and swell as he holds the plates, his chest pumps up.

You're feeding off it! I yell: Look at you! Look at you!

Now, Maggie, Jonah says: Calm down.

Send them away! I don't want them here. The two of you—selling refreshments at my sideshow.

Maggie, Jonah says, and hangs his head.

Mose puts down the plates of food. He glances out the window a long while. He says: Did you ever come see 'bout me? When you was happy? All those years, Maggie, did you come?

Mose looks at me plainly, sharp as a knife. He continues: Even when Papa passed?

I sent a card, I mumble.

He nods: I was obliged. But did you come see 'bout me, Maggie?

Jonah shifts, uncomfortable in his seat. Mose calls to him: Jonah, you ever set to my table before?

Jonah and I look at one another. I know what he thinks about. All those nights sitting on my sofa, drinking beer, me, Dizzy, and Jonah. Them teasing me. About dating corny Mose Job. His flannel shirts. His highwaters. His short, nappy hair always a little too matted to his head and not unknown to hold lint. While I protested some, it was never wholehearted. I never said that Mose used to hold me on a soft blanket in these fields and listen to my problems, tell me my feet weren't too big when I wore a size-eleven shoe at five foot, five inches tall. That we used to meet and maul each other, hungry, like teenagers do, just shy of real sex but still, he was my lover. I didn't say any of that. I just laughed along.

I was something to you once, Mose says so softly and clearly: I thought you'd know. You, of everybody. You'd know how it'd be for me here. Did you ever think of me, Maggie?

Wanna run. But held tight here somehow. Though I struggle to get free.

Now, you see how it is. All that water rushing at you. Maybe it was just me, all dammed up here. Maybe it could've been me let loose. That's what I dreamt last night. That I stole 'em from you. That I swept you back to me.

I run now from the house. Down the field. I know I am followed. I hear the click of cameras; bulbs flash and pop and crackle behind me—I'm a wild giraffe at safari—into the creek, stumbling up on the shore, down the marsh through Felbo's field, double back through the barn, scattering the chickens and the few pigs that survive. Bar the door, panting, holding my belly. They bang outside: Maggie, Maggie, Maggie. I squat and cover my face in my hands.

That's how they find me, how they take my photo over and again. I never look up, even when they prod me and nudge me, when they put their arms around me to coax me. There is nothing to coax. Nothing to say. Their words are all a drone, a toneless, flat line.

Mose and Jonah come for me. Felbo helps run off the reporters. In the squad car nobody talks. I look up at Mose for the first time and look away quick. When we're far away from everybody I tell Jonah to stop the car. He turns around to me.

I wanna walk from here, I say. Mose, I whisper: I wanna go to our place.

Jonah frowns. Mose says: We'll be all right.

We get out of the car and walk slowly. It's dusk now—I still can't tell how time passes. I reach for Mose's scaly hand. He gives it freely.

Back to the place, my place, past the gooey mud that peels off sections of the Baptist Church, peels it perfectly pew by pew like slices of cake. Back to my tree in this place near my salvation. I didn't even think of God when It happened. He never crossed my mind in those terrible moments. I look at Mose behind me on the blacktop. Sitting upright and watching me. I wait for him to take his place. He does not. I see that he won't. So I grab my tree alone. I dangle in water which is nearly still now. Mose stands up, hands in his pockets. He paces slowly, sometimes dragging a foot through small pools of water. When he looks at me, patient and kind, he smiles, then goes back to pacing. But he is different now standing on his blacktop. He's distant. He looks at it not as he did—not as if it were his own skin or nail, not the way he once looked at it, like each rocky crater of the ground was his own, like every scent it expelled bore his own breath. No. It is separate now and he looks away from it and stubs his toe against it and feels nothing. So, I am alone here on my tree, in this river. He sweeps by, sweeps his foot on the blacktop over and over, scraping off whatever residue it holds of him. I dangle here in this river. Unbearably alone. Tired. Tired. And then I let go.

A clean fall down. Does my head go underwater? I cannot tell. I am too filled with relief—this is how it feels. Now I know, taken suddenly, surely. I give over. But the water barely moves now. There is time to see it happen. There is time to touch the shore, to memorize its crags and gaping dark holes, the long tentacles of tree roots exposed. There is time for Mose to catch me. He dives in, and I am furious. He pulls me to him and I think to fight and flail, to push his puny body away. A small core of me rebels. But my body goes limp against him. In front of us, a metal chain looped around a tree hangs long into the water. He drags me to it and grabs on, lacing his knobby fingers through the metal loops, hooking on with tenacity, scraping his knuckles to force his fingers, a tight fit. All the while I am lifeless and heavy, and he whispers to me: Don't go.

We drift here and the chain pulls taut. I watch his finger bend and then break in the loop, popping backwards. Still, he clutches me, his eyes shut tight; he whispers: Don't leave me. When the headlights shine on us, I see the blood that gushes from Mose's fingers, three rivers of dark blood from the rusty chain. Jonah Kind brings a rope to the edge of the river: Jesus Christ! he yells. First, I am saved. And then Mose. I sink against the police car, my belly tight and hard, contracting. Mose comes to me and I grab his broken hand. Press hard on the flesh to seal it, to stop the flow of his blood. I press it to my lips and push down hard on his cold flesh.

What the hell you two doing down here? Jonah says, more frightened than mad: I decided to follow you this time—good thing, too! What d'ya wanna do, die out here?

I stare at Mose's jagged skin. He sighs: No.

I wail and this current flows from me, sudden and warm. The water I held, stingy, lets loose from my womb. My baby, I moan: It's coming now.

They stand and look at each other a moment, as if they had not known I was pregnant. As if the risk of being with a pregnant woman wasn't birth. Finally, Jonah coughs: Shit! And they lift me to my feet, help me into the backseat of the car. I cannot sit upright. My pains come fast and hard, my body opens itself. I feel my pelvic bones soften and slide. I feel the head bearing down.

It's coming fast, I say.

Jonah looks at Mose and frowns: What the hell's that mean?

Means drive, Mose says.

I am! Jonah snaps.

Drive faster.

Jonah rubs his forehead and speeds, the tail end of the car sliding out on the mud-slick road. I reach up and slap him on the shoulder: Heah! Watch it, Jonah! I say.

Grass and rotting corn stalks rise like the sea, lapping at the car windows. A big yellow moon hangs low, skimming the grassy waves. We skid. Damn, damn, Jonah says, and cuts his wheel hard. Mose reaches back and puts a hand on my knee, which points in the air while I lay on my back. We skid in a figure eight, zigzagging on the road, Jonah swearing and whipping the wheel back and forth. We veer off the road to the left and land square in the mud. Jonah spins his wheels awhile, then slaps the dashboard: Shit! Shit! Shit!

We are rutted deep. Back where I began.

My baby's head pushes its way out of me. Mose, Mose, I moan. He climbs into the backseat with me.

How the hell can it come so fast? Jonah asks: Doesn't this usually take days?

None of my babies took days, and this is my third.

It's a long time coming anyway, Mose says.

Other than my panting, there is no sound. No wind, and if the river rushes, I cannot hear it. Jonah looks terrified, sweating and swallowing hard.

Pull the front seats all the way up, Mose says to him. He slips off my underpants, yanks them down quickly over my hips. One of my legs he lifts and drapes over the back of the front seat. Jonah gets out and paces. I can run for h-h-help, he says.

Mose shakes his head: Jonah, you are the help.

It's coming fast, I say, and hang my head back: I don't know if I can do this again.

Mose lifts my head: There's never "again." Nothing's ever just the same. You know. Jonah, c'mon now. Hold her head up.

Jonah shakes his head fast and for a moment looks about to weep. I've never done this, he says: I–I–I don't even have a girlfriend.

Cradle her head, Mose says.

Help me push up, I command.

Jonah bends in the mud, his cold hands on my shoulders, his cheek against the back of my head so I feel him tremble.

This baby tears its way from me. When I bear down, half sitting up and supported by Jonah, I see the naked moon, round and bald as a newborn's head. Does this child know how it enters? They sweep by me grabbing, grabbing. I hold on.

I bear down: Mose, I call. And he gives me his hand, his fingers bent and crooked and dried with blood. Beautiful. I moan and out it comes in a sudden bloody rush—it goes so fast, out like a surfer atop a fast wave. It shoots straight for Mose, his face bright in moonlight. He drops my hand and grabs at the baby, which bounces high and slow. Oh, God, Jonah moans in my ear: Oh, Dizzy! Oh, Mother!

Mose fumbles the baby, a cagey, slippery fish wriggling off his line. The three of us are held here—Jonah, Mose, and me, the only three in the world—we pause in the stillness of high grass and mud. This time I am prepared for what I will lose. I am steeled. If this is the last of mine, I will just close this place in me, seal myself as a house, peer out until my view grows too dusty and obscured.

Mose fumbles. My baby fights his grasp. Mose's hands open wide and sure. He leans in and catches the baby in his arms, against his chest. My baby girl rears back yelping and squirming. He sighs.

The stench that invades Ladyslipper subsides, overwhelmed by fresh blood and tissue. My baby screams her claim to existence. Mose rests her on my belly and cradles her slimy hips. Jonah strokes her perfect round head. In these swollen fields, in this moonlight grace, we are spared.

Short-Story Award for New Writers

1st-, 2nd-, and 3rd-Place Winners

1st place and $1200 to *Lance Weller*, for "The Breathable Air"

Weller's profile appears on page 40 and his story begins on page 41.

2nd place and $500 to *Catherine Seto*, for "The Other"

Catherine Seto is a twenty-four-year-old fiction writer who lives in Ann Arbor, Michigan. She holds an MFA in fiction from the University of Michigan and is currently working on a novel.

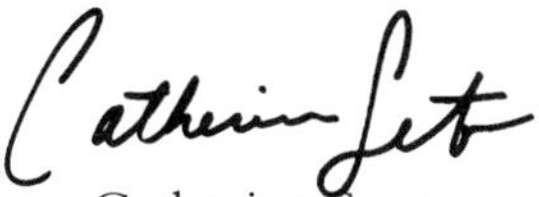

Catherine Seto

"The Other"

Poy's face would be titled Five Muddy Points: scissor-point eyebrows, wall-less nose, knuckles without eyes, buggy lips, shallow throat. These forecasted the doom in a person's destiny, from poverty and dishonesty to dying an early and painful death.

3rd place and $300 to *Jennifer Tseng*, for "My Mother's Country"

Jennifer Tseng is currently finishing her MA in Asian-American studies at UCLA. Soon she'll be teaching her first class, "Imagining History: Chinese American History from a Literary Perspective." "My Mother's Country" is part of a collection of stories, poems and fragments entitled *The S & Other Stories.*

Jennifer Tseng

"My Mother's Country"

Without my father here to punctuate our relationship, the world could not see who we were together.

We thank all entrants for sending in their work.

Lance Weller

We were the best of friends when I was growing up, although there were some days when I think she had trouble tolerating me.

This is Lance Weller's first published story. He has no formal training in writing but has been doing it all his life. As a child, Weller would turn episodes of *The Twilight Zone* and *The Outer Limits* into stories on his grandmother's typewriter. He has finished one novel, titled *Any Other Boy*, and has high hopes for it. Weller is thirty-two and likes dogs.

LANCE WELLER

The Breathable Air

FIRST-PLACE WINNER
Short-Story Award
for New Writers

She can see vast distances.

Plains. And on the edges of the plains, hills purple beneath a blue sky. A city in white on the foreground. Cypress trees. Torch flames. The sun bright and the shape of the wind described by the bend and clash of green grasses. These and other colors that have no correlation to the hues of the living world around her—she sees with something other than her eyes.

She can hear the smallest sounds.

His voice is at her ear, constant and familiar and comforting in its steadfast devotion, but it is not the voice to which she listens. There is another voice, closer and in contest with his. Stories read from old books of times so far removed she has trouble comprehending them at first. Once, and long ago, she wrote books like this. She decides the other voice is her own, finishing for her some last and half-imagined tale.

In the mild, blue-black shade of a tiny grape arbor just inside the entrance to Vincente Coruscuito's courtyard garden in the city of Padua, Year of Our Lord 1348, Leonardo Monclavo stood awaiting the arrival of his love, Katarina Novali.

It was a late spring day and hot, though he could still feel the soft breezes that blew across the long grassy plains from the coast and taste upon them the rich spices of sea salt and unplowed soil. Like landward trades, he thought, stepping into the sun to mark the time by the angle of his raised arm's shadow upon a flat stone nearby. He lowered his arm and frowned, then looked up at the sun where it burned low-slung and white upon the tiled rooftops. Frowning, Leonardo went to the heavy oak door that barred his friend Vincente's garden from the street, and with one finger raised a square leather flap and peered out through the spy-hole.

No one moved on the street this time of day and the dust raised by the little winds fell slowly in clouds flecked with gold. From somewhere came hoarse cries of lamentation—shrieking, sexless sounds neutered by the deep cut of grief. And then, as if in answer, the bells in the basilica began a heavy, echoing toll.

It seemed the bells sounded constantly now with plague afoot in Padua, and that very morning Leonardo had himself seen a group of becchini carrying the dead to church. Ragged men, they carried, balanced on their shoulders, an old door upon which they had stacked several bodies like sheaves of grain. The faces of the dead, seized by their sickness and bearing its sign upon their flesh, beheld the sun aghast as though in their dying they had been shown some certain thing that none should ever see. Leonardo had seen the corpse-carriers coming, watched how they scanned doorways with their small, malignant eyes, looking for marks of soap upon the panels to signify the dead or dying within. He had stepped into an alley until they passed, then hurried on to his friend's garden, noting with some relief the lack of soap upon the garden door, though Vincente Coruscuito lay abed and had not risen these past three days.

As Leonardo looked out through the spy-hole for Katarina Novali, or for some sign of her, a dog padded noiselessly across his field of vision—a huge, black mastiff with one rent ear leaking slow blood down its withers to its chest. The animal paused in its course and looked up at the door where Leonardo stood watching. From its wet jaws hung pale and limp a small left hand. A signet ring upon the forefinger winked in the sun, and loose skin, like the emptied sleeve of a blouse, depended from the gnawed wrist in intricate filigree. The dog did not growl nor raise its hackles, but moved its head from side to side as though to display more fully the prize it had scavenged. Leonardo saw the fingers twitching, like the legs of an obscenely fat white spider, as the dog's teeth plucked and pressed at tendons. After a time it raised its head to scent the air, looked at him once more, then took small sidelong steps down the street and away. As the bells' echo drifted in the silence of the afternoon, Leonardo shuddered and stepped back from the door to reenter the shade of the vines.

He wiped his eyes and breathed hard to catch breath, and looked about at the garden. He saw it as an Eden bulwarked by dusty clay walls against the Gehenna of the city. He saw there, in the garden, meandering footpaths of cobblestone aproned by green grass and small shrubberies from which plump, dark currants drooped. Sprays of fern, splashed bright by hollyhock, traced emerald frescoes 'round the walls, while stands of small blue teacup flowers shivered in the shade of the olive tree. Arabesques of vine and tendril spilled down the walls, and all of it—leaf and petal and stamen and pistil, grassblade, the mist of pollen swirling in the air, the lazy passages of bees from flower to flower—lent the place a sense of depth, of health. As though there was no scourge laying the dead out in their own dooryards, nor could there ever be. Leonardo stood there, idly scratching a fleabite on his neck, and breathed deeply of the rich, vegetative perfumes and smelled also, faintly, the reek of bodies putrefying in the streets outside the garden walls.

He glanced up to Vincente's window. It overlooked the garden and stood open, the curtains limp, still wet from the maid's soaking, to cool the air within and keep the pestilence without. Now, a small rat sat cleaning itself upon the sill and Leonardo glanced about for a stone to throw, but when he looked back, the rat had vanished.

In one corner of the garden stood a fountain in the shape of an open clamshell and painted the color of lapis. Vincente had brought it home with him from a visit to Tuscany. Stalks of spearmint swayed in the breeze at either side and cast fluted shadows through the trembling water. Little sunset-colored fishes, unfed for days now by their master, plashed about within the shell in sounds sudden and musical to Leonardo's ears.

Upon a small wooden table set out in the shade of the olive was a half-loaf of bread gone green with mold and gnawed and pecked by rats and birds. Leonardo realized he heard no birds singing now and wondered over that. He had been told by a trader from Almeria how in Messina the birds themselves had fallen, stricken, from the sky. How cats and dogs, monkeys, asses, even deer in the forest were said to exhibit the same buboes as men, but Leonardo did not know the truth of that. The image of the black hound with its awful trophy came to him and Leonardo shuddered deeply, then stooped to scratch along the inside of his thigh where his skin had grown hot and wet with stale sweat.

He crossed to the table and took up the loaf in his hands and broke it open to scatter crumbs into the fountain. The fish rose, slow at first, gaping with ceaseless stares at the solid world above them as their mouths groped the underside of the water. They ate and he watched them for a time, wishing he had brought wine with him to quench the dryness of his throat.

Looking at the falling sun again, he frowned and stretched, feeling deep aches across his chest and down his legs. Judging time once more by his arm's cast shadow, he wagered Katarina Novali's handmaiden had not read his last letter to her. Or he hoped it. The image of his love in her immaculateness stretched out upon the stoop of a doorway, fly-besotted, waiting for the becchini to carry her off to a common grave, gave him more pain than his muscles did as he shook them loose. But soon he calmed himself from that thought. He remembered the first time he had seen her, when the plague was still an ugly rumor used to frighten disobedient children. Katarina Novali had been walking down the street near the university, her hand balanced lightly on the forearm of her maid, her face an open smile and her eyes completely sightless. Leonardo had paused with his books to watch her approach and was still standing there, watching the dust her feet had made settle, long after she had disappeared in the crowd.

And now, to ease his mind around her tardiness, Leonardo reasoned that the pestilence could not touch her due to the very fact of her blindness. At the university he studied science, medicine, and had heard it said that the plague was a corruption of the atmosphere. But, though it traveled by the medium of air like a vapor, it was through the eyes that it entered the human body, for it is through vision that men first sin against God. The first victims in Padua were walled up within their own homes so they should not gaze upon their healthy neighbors and thereby infect them. But no sin was too small for the pestilence to overlook and soon it made a kingdom of the city. The professors advised their students never to look the dying man in the eyes lest the sickness enter the one who treats him. It was good advice and from it Leonardo was consoled that his love could not fall victim.

He cleared his throat and leaned and spat an evil-tasting humor upon the flagstones near the fountain, then stepped behind the olive tree to relieve himself. His water fell weakly from him, without force, and splashed the tops of his boots. As he leaned back against the trunk to fasten his breeches, his fingertips brushed something he had not felt when he scratched earlier. He swallowed dryly and lifted his shirt to look.

He closed his eyes and with effort calmed the breath that

rattled up hot and sudden within him. Looking back down, he winced to see the bubo swelling dark and venomous beside his sex. Leonardo's fingers trembled as he touched it, then prodded it. The lump was unyielding—round and hard and hot as a bird's egg boiled. Touching it forced a hot stab of pain down his legs and across his buttocks.

He quickly fastened back up and, limping somewhat from the sudden pain, returned to the place near the fountain where he had spat. It seemed to sizzle there on the sun-hot stone, dark with blood. Leonardo stared down at what had come up from inside him, and it stared back cruel and black and impassive as the eye of the dog. He sat heavily beside the fountain and one hand slipped into the water. He felt a fish swim away from his palm like quick silk through his fingers. After a time he began to weep and was weeping still when he heard a knocking upon the garden door.

Lawrence Kelman's reading voice slowly trailed away to silence and he gently closed the book of poems he had been reading to his wife. He looked at Elsabeth where she lay sleeping—perhaps dreaming, but of what he had no way to know. Setting the thick book down on her night table, he folded his hands across his stomach and watched her. The blankets rose and fell and, with her eyes closed in sleep, he could see the faint traces of the girl's face, the woman's that he had once known. He felt his own eyes grow heavy and liquid as they tracked the passage of her years in care-lines carved about her mouth, about her eyes. Since the stroke, her lips had become so thin and bloodless they seemed an afterthought to her face, and he realized that it had been more than five months since he had heard her speak. Lawrence knew, suddenly and with absolute surety, that if he heard her voice now in some other setting, standing in line at the supermarket for instance, he would not recognize it, and he was ashamed of himself.

And, as he always did after reading to her every night, he wondered could she hear him at all. Or did she know his own voice, or the careful touch of the back of his hand against her cheek, the brush of his lips against her forehead? Her eyes, when they were open, gave him no sign, explained nothing of the inner workings of her mind or body. Hard and dark as split shells, they stared passively at whatever he might turn her face toward, and only rarely did he see her blink. It was as though the stroke had dried to straw some essential fiber deep within her. When he bathed her with a soft, moist towel while she lay limp, pale upon the bed—the covers turned back neatly, smoothed with careful precision under the flat of his palm, the water in the basin warmed and tested by the back of his wrist like with a baby's bottle—her skin seemed to drink the water, quenching some deep impossible thirst through every pore.

And now she slept and Lawrence watched her, as he always did, before going to his own bed. In her sleep, Elsabeth's neck became once more a supple, elegant curve of white flesh that rose from a collarbone standing from her breast like a pair of stiff wings. Sleep worked small wonders about her person and for it he was grateful.

He listened to the sound of her breath, contrapuntal to the sound of the rain drumming the roof, running in the gutters, and falling through the downspouts of their small home. He reached out and switched off the lamp at bedside and watched rain-glazed patterns of light and shadow form and disperse and collect again in little archipelagic shapes that drifted slowly down the walls, as cars on the street outside swept headlights through the room. In those patterns he imagined other worlds entire—seas of warm yellow light, reefs of soft shadow, islands of darkness—and he imagined the two of them, he and Elsabeth, living in those worlds. Merely the two of them—whole and healthy and far from the rest of this world. After a time, when he knew that she was deep in her sleep, Lawrence leaned over his wife to kiss her forehead before making his way across the hall to his own room.

In the morning, Lawrence rose with the sun's first light, as was his custom. He began to cough. He coughed for a very long time, and when it was over he went to the bathroom to rinse his mouth out. He looked into the sink and made a face, then heaved a great sigh and swirled the waste down the drain. He went into the kitchen to sip at a cup of coffee while he watched through the window. Monday morning, and motorists on their way to work passed on the street with their coffee mugs balanced on their dashboards and grim expressions fixed on their faces. A few joggers went by, their shoulders glazed with sweat under the late spring's sun. The light of that sun angled down through the kitchen window and lay upon the table like honey spread thick on bread. Lawrence put his hands on the table and let the sun warm them until he noticed a subtle change in the atmosphere of the house. As though the air that had sat heavy and dull and warm throughout the night had suddenly quickened and begun to move again, and Lawrence knew that Elsabeth was awake.

He went into the front room where shelves of books adorned every available wall space. Elsabeth's books on Renaissance Italy had a shelf to themselves, and Lawrence reached out and let his fingertips trail across their spines, her name in gilt beside each title. He had taken off the dustjackets after she had been confined to her bed, because he found himself staring at her pictures on each paper cover and trying to remember what it had been like while she was still able to write. He touched as well the dog-eared manuscript pages of the novel she had never finished, and sighed heavily.

Through the window he could see the hanging fuchsia baskets on the front porch still wet with rainwater from the night just passed. The sun sparkled on the slick, glistening leaves and the funneled corollas trembled in the small breezes tossed up against the side of the house by passing cars. A dog came down the sidewalk and Lawrence paused to watch it. It was a mixed breed and white in its coloring. He saw that it limped, holding its right foreleg cocked against its chest, and it was painfully thin. It stopped just opposite where he stood within the house watching, and raised its head, as though it did not know which way to go next and so must ponder in its own way the course to take. Lawrence watched it scent the air, its wet mouth open. For a moment the dog looked in his direction, and its eyes were brown and large and soft there in the sun. Then it looked back down and went slowly on with its abbreviated three-footed gait.

He went to Elsabeth and told her good morning and set her coffee on the night table. She had not drunk coffee for months now, but he brought her a cup anyway, as though some morning she might reach for it. She stared at the ceiling where her face was pointed, and breathed. He talked to her of little things as he drew back the covers carefully and prepared to change her soiled diaper. He recomposed for her his dreams from his last night's sleeping and asked after her own, and she was silent, and he fell silent too while cleaning her, and together they were quiet in the morning's coolness.

When the phone rang he scowled and waited for the machine to pick it up. He sat his wife up in her bed and eased her arms through the sleeves of a clean blouse and heard from the kitchen the sound of his own voice on the message-tape, curt and rough and weary, and then the doctor's nurse. Lawrence lay Elsabeth back down and held her hand as he listened to the woman remind him of tomorrow morning. What time the car would come for her, what things he should have ready, how he could visit her the next day. "After we get her settled in her new environment," said the nurse. "After that, you can visit her there every day … during posted hours of course." Her voice was soft, apologetic.

When she had finished speaking and hung up, Lawrence

walked into the kitchen and lifted the smoked plastic lid of the answering machine. He took the cassette out, stood over the garbage can in the laundry room, and very methodically unspooled the tape into the garbage. When he was done, he looked at the nest of destroyed tape atop that morning's coffee grounds and shook his head. "Goddamn it anyway," he said.

It took Lawrence ten minutes of rooting around in the back of a drawer to find the replacement tape for the answering machine. He snapped it into place and closed the lid, then, before he could record a new message, remembered Elsabeth and how he had left her sitting up. He went back to the bedroom and saw she had fallen asleep that way. He watched her for a very long time, willing himself to remember always the sound of her sleeping breath, then turned to go into the kitchen to hunt up some scraps for the dog he'd seen.

They were the same four that Leonardo had seen earlier that morning, only now instead of carrying on their shoulders a door, they had appropriated a little wooden trundle cart which they wheeled before them, stacked with grisly cargo. When he opened the door to their knocking, the becchini pushed past him without speaking and crossed the garden to enter the house proper. From where he stood, Leonardo could see Vincente's maid within the darkness of the house motioning the men toward the stairs.

Leonardo blinked and swallowed. It caused him a little pain, and he became aware of his shoulders shaking slightly. He was very hot and the bubo at his groin seemed to sizzle in his flesh, burning him with every movement, every insuck of breath. He glanced out into the street at the corpse-carriers' wheelbarrow. There were three bodies in it: a man of middle-age, a woman most likely his wife, and a boy-child of about five years. Tumors swelled blackly on their faces, necks, and arms. Their skin was stretched and crazed and split. Flies explored the air about them and Leonardo looked closer to see the child's left hand missing and the ragged, bloody marks of claw and tooth about his person.

The four becchini came back out of the house. Two walked unencumbered, but behind them Leonardo saw the second pair dragging his friend's body by the arms. Vincente had once been a large man, big-boned and fleshy. Now he was all sharp angles and bone jutting out against his soiled nightclothes. His flesh bore the same ruptures and buboes as the family in the cart, and Leonardo stared at him and began to tremble. He covered his mouth with his hand and looked away as the two becchini heaved Vincente Coruscuito up and into the deadcart where he lay staring heavenward with a fixed expression of something like mirth. As though Death had paused to relate some colorful tale which Vincente found amusing.

The leader of the four noticed him then and realized that Leonardo was not another servant. The man was small and thin and dirty and the whites of his eyes had a yellow cast to them. The becchini was unshaven and when he smiled Leonardo saw dark blossomings of rot working at his teeth.

"Young gentleman," said the becchini. "Young gentleman, do you know this work we do?"

The air seemed very bright, and Leonardo had to squint to make the other out, and saw him as a swath of dark, like a shadow untouched by sunlight. He swallowed and grimaced over the pain at the back of his throat, and told him that he did.

"Then you would know how thirsty a work it is, then. Wouldn't you?" He fixed him with a questioning stare until Leonardo mumbled that he did.

"Have you then, young sir, coin to give poor working folk?" The becchini tilted his head to the side and put his palm up between them. Behind the man, his fellows muttered amongst themselves and shuffled their boots in the hot dust. Leonardo saw they all wore daggers at their belts and one took his out to whittle idly at the cart handle.

He drew four coins from a pouch at his breast and dropped them in the becchini's hand. The little man's eyes widened, and then he grinned and took a step back to look Leonardo up and down. Pocketing the coins, he placed a finger to the side of one eye and said, "You're a student."

Leonardo nodded.

"And you are waiting in a dead man's garden when nearly all students have fled Padua. It must be that you are in love."

Leonardo blinked to get the other in focus. "How can you know that?"

The becchini touched his own caved chest with the tips of his splayed fingers. "I once attended a university. I was once in love. Did you think that one such as myself could not? Did you think me perhaps born to this filthy trade?" He waved a hand at Leonardo. "No matter. It is no matter at all for now I am indeed only that which you see before you."

"What happened? Why do you do this?" Leonardo nodded to the deadcart, the bodies ripening in the sun with Vincente now among them. He could see the signs of bloat in the child's face and neck—a dark swelling there as though he held his breath.

The man sucked a tooth and shook his head. "Because it is a necessary thing to do, young sir. You ask me what and you ask me why and in so doing you ask me for a story, my story, and I am not inclined to tell it. The moments of my life leading to this moment are mine alone and I'll not tell them, save that the one I loved was not strong. She did not survive the pestilence and I did. And I was still strong enough to carry her to her grave afterward, and bear the look upon her face as I shoveled dirt over it. I was strong enough to do that and I am strong enough to do this." He gestured to the bodies behind him. "And in that I am happy."

Leonardo shook his head. "I do not understand you, sir."

The becchini grinned wide to reveal his awful teeth

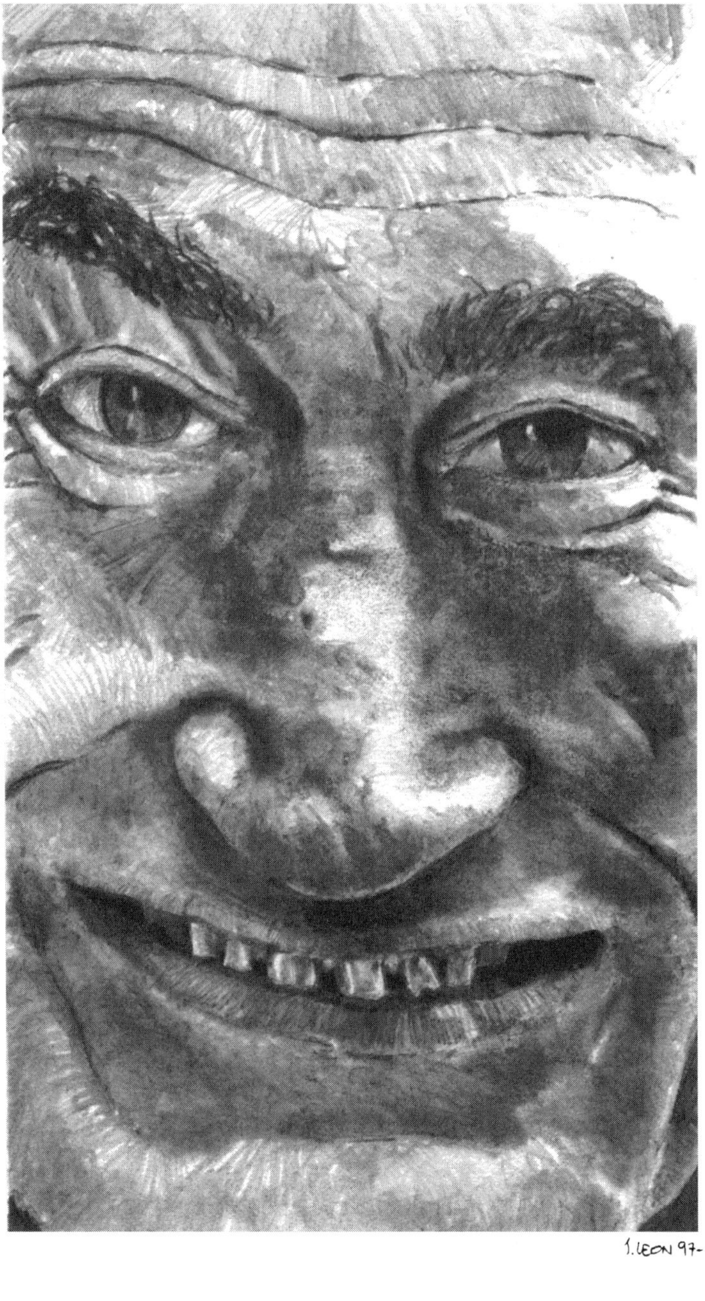
J. LEON 97-

and said, "A man might search his life away for something meaningful—success perhaps. But joy is in doing the thing that's needed at the moment, and doing it well and without fear and with something like love."

They stood silent together for some moments. The bells began to sound again. Overhead, Leonardo saw a hawk stitching the sky in long loops. When he looked back down, the becchini and his men were moving off down the street. They had lit torches to keep the pestilence at bay with smoke, and the man with whom Leonardo had spoken turned and called, "Your lady love ... where does she live?"

Leonardo shouted out the quarter of the city where Katarina Novali lived with her father, and the becchini shook his head slowly from side to side. "No one remains. They've all left the city days ago and every house is empty."

Leonardo stared. The becchini shrugged and turned to rejoin his fellows. Leonardo stood in the failing sun watching after them and listening to the sound of the cart groaning down the street, and the sudden, high call of the hawk, and the softening echo of the bells, until finally there was only the slow, low moan of the wind pushing through the alleys. He turned and shut the garden door, locked it with a brass key, then threw the key over the wall and walked away.

Leonardo wandered through the streets for hours in despair over his life, but at the same time joyous that his only love had most likely reached the safety of the countryside. The afternoon sun blended smoothly into twilight and torches were lit all about the city, though Leonardo encountered no other soul walking in the streets. There were several times he had to lean against a wall to catch his breath. His lungs burned and his joints ached. Once, in an alley strewn with garbage and the bodies of dead livestock, he fell to his hands and knees to vomit dark blood. At the university, he had seen the sick sometimes die in the space of a day, and there was not a thing that could be done once the black blood came spewing from their stomachs.

In the purple of eventide a cool wind bore down upon Padua, freshening the air and making the torch flames gambol. Leonardo hobbled from shadow to shadow and arrived, finally, at an empty stable. There were old soap marks on the door and the stalls had all been turned open. The gutted carcass of a swine lay in a thatch of blood-soaked straw and the smell of dung was sour. From the doorway, Leonardo could see a line of cypress trees that marked the edge of the campus, and he watched as they bent and clashed and creaked as the wind twisted through them. He watched out the door for a time, then turned and went inside. He kicked straw into a corner of a stall and lay down upon it.

His eyes were hot and burning in their fleshy orbits, and his heart knocked loud and trembled spastic in its cage of bone. He was very weak and when he vomited again it was all he could do to simply turn his head. He closed his eyes. He could hear the smallest sounds: someone coughing wetly from the house next door, flies returning to their carrion nests for the night, his pores tightening, dry with thirst.

When he slivered his eyes open, Leonardo had no way to know how long the mastiff had been watching him. It was a black shape just without the stall door, and it was utterly silent but for breath. It raised its hackles but Leonardo could not see its eyes for darkness. With effort, he lifted his head and rolled onto his back. He tasted warm blood, metallic in his mouth, and old blood dried to a crust about his lips. The bubo at his groin split suddenly as he shifted and bathed his thighs with warmth. He was aware he felt little pain. The black hound watched him as he slid his little knife from his belt. Leonardo held it with the butt of the pommel resting on his stomach. He could see the blade in the dark. The dog began to growl: a low sound, ancient in its intent. Leonardo sniffed and swallowed hard. With his free hand, he beckoned the dog and it came forward quickly, silent again, its teeth moon-colored in the dark, its wet mouth open.

When he woke, Lawrence looked at his watch and swore. The day was nearly gone and he stood from the couch. He began to cough, but it was not so bad, and he quieted after a minute or two. He swallowed the thick phlegm grimly and went down the hall to check on Elsabeth. She was still asleep and he thanked God for small favors and went out onto the porch. The little dish of table scraps was empty and he scanned the wooded lot next door for signs of the dog, but there were none.

He was inside, filling a water dish to put outside for the dog, when the phone rang. Lawrence set the dish down and ran his damp hands down the thighs of his trousers as he crossed to the phone, but the machine picked it up before he could reach it. He stopped in the middle of the kitchen and stared at the floor.

"You've reached the Kelman residence." Elsabeth's voice from maybe five years ago. "We're unable to come to the phone at the moment—" A squeal of feedback, then Lawrence heard himself laughing and remembered the day. Elsabeth said, "Oh, damn machine!" and then a hiss of static as the tape spun itself apart inside the machine.

The caller had already hung up, and Lawrence opened the lid and lifted free the destroyed cassette. He stood there, as the day darkened into evening, holding the tape in his palm, staring at it. He took it into the living room and sat down on the couch. When it was full dark, he left the tape on the coffee table and went into her room.

At first he tried to read to her from the book of poems he'd left on her table the night before. But he couldn't concentrate on the words or their cadence, and so held her frail hand a while instead. He looked at the way the hand was just beginning to curl in on itself, the way a bird hides its head beneath a wing, and he looked at her face. "I don't know what I'm supposed to do," he told her.

"You tell me what to do."

Elsabeth stared at the ceiling and Lawrence switched off the light. He could see her eyes in the dark, her parted lips, her teeth. Her hair a shadowy net upon the pillow that caught his words and held them near her head. Understood or not. After a while he stood.

With shaking hands he removed his clothes and lay them neatly across the chairback until he stood naked beside her bed. There was a moon out and its light played upon his pale body so he felt he glowed, that he had become the ghost of himself already. He fixed his mind around not coughing. Elsabeth's breath was even, untroubled.

He got slowly into bed with her but did not know how to feel. He lay for a long time beside her, feeling her fierce warmth against his upper arm; then he moved his hand to touch her stomach, his palm flat to feel the breath entering and leaving and entering again. He fumbled with the buttons of her blouse and pressed his face against her hair. He found her mouth with his and his hands moved gently on her body. Pressing against her thigh he curled her fingers around himself and held them there with one hand as his hips rocked. He imagined her awake with her nimble, strong fingers cupped, then clenched, and imagined also those little islands and reefs of light, of shadow, of darkness. The two of them together there, and happy.

In the end he wept. Because it was no good and he could not finish; because it was the last time he would share a bed with his wife; because he had heard her voice that evening and not recognized it. He wept because he was not privy to her dreams or the life of her imagination, nor she to his, and he wept for the final passing of their life together, and because they were each so utterly alone now.

Sometime after midnight, Lawrence Kelman woke and rose from the bed. The night was quiet—no rain nor traffic on the street. Moonlight spilt through the window and touched here and there about the room. He braced himself to cough, but it didn't come, and he stood in the center of the room feeling a lightness of spirit he'd not felt in many months. Though Elsabeth lay sleeping in her bed, the house seemed empty, and he moved from room to room touching things like a haunt come back to a memory. He went into his own room and stood at the open window looking at the wooded lot next door.

The dog moved slowly through the trees like the ghost of a dog. Lawrence stood very still and held his breath. The animal crossed the yard and stood at the bottom porch step, staring at him before finally limping up the steps and bending its head over the water dish. It drank and turned three tight circles before settling down on the porch-boards to sleep under Lawrence's watching eye. He stood there a long time, watching it rest. He thought it was the most beautiful thing he'd seen in a very long time.

She cannot see clearly for the dark. Nor is there much sound. Perhaps the ticking of the clock she and Lawrence had brought home from Italy, or the soft creak of the floorboards where they sagged in the hall. Perhaps her own breath across her teeth. There is a swath of moonlight slanting through the window to her left and another yellow rind of light to her right. In that yellow light something moves, and she dreams she turns her head to see him standing at his bedroom window naked, watching something and taking delight in it. He is silhouetted there and his skin is marbled in light, smooth. His shoulders are wide and strong.

Then come dreams rife with the possibilities of endings. Perhaps she dies that moment, happy, or merely falls asleep once more. Perhaps they are bricked-up together, man and wife, within a house in Padua and perhaps no pestilence comes upon them. Or, perhaps, she rises from the bed and goes to him where he stands and together they watch the day break.

There is a voice that tells her there are no endings nor were there ever. That endings by their definition imply a void, and so things must go on much the same as they ever were in Padua or elsewhere, for lovers and for maidens, and for husbands and for wives. She decides it is her own voice. She can hear the smallest sounds. She can see very far.

Kevin Canty

Going someplace, showing off, with what appears to be a bad wig on my head. That's my brother in the backseat, I think.

Kevin Canty's first novel, *Into the Great Wide Open*, was published by Nan A. Talese/Doubleday. Canty is also the author of a collection of stories titled *A Stranger in This World* (Doubleday, 1994; Vintage, 1995). His short fiction has appeared in *Esquire*, *Story*, *Glimmer Train Stories*, *New England Review*, and *Missouri Review*.

Canty teaches writing at the University of Montana in Missoula, where he lives with his wife, Lucy Capeheart, and their children, Turner and Nora.

Kevin Canty

Little Debbie

I know what she's dreaming about: chocolate cakes and strawberry pies, french fries and ice cream, whipped cream, custard cream, Devonshire cream and buttered toast. I know what turns her on. It makes me jealous sometimes.

I'm sitting in the ladder-back chair next to our bed and I'm, say, tipsy, and I'm watching her body rise and fall with her breathing. The light is coming through the open window from the yard lamp, blue. I'm listening to the crickets. It's the end of summer, still too hot to have the house opened up, but Deb doesn't like to be cooped up in the AC. She sleeps with just a sheet on under the big fan, nothing on but a pair of white panties that make her look even more tan than she is, and the sheet is twisted around and rumpled so it doesn't cover much. It's better than *Playboy*.

The trouble starts when she wakes up. She pulls the sheet up over her and says, What are you looking at?

I'm looking at you.

Don't, she says. Cut it out. I was *sleeping*.

Go back to sleep. I didn't mean to wake you.

You go on, she says—and then a minute later, when I'm still around, she says it again. Go on! I don't like it.

What?

When you look at me like that.

Like what?

She doesn't say anything, just stares at me with her arms folded tight against her ribs, holding that sheet against her, tight. There's nothing for me here. There's nothing for me in the living room, either, which is how I got here in the first place. But it's either that or go to bed and lie there in the dark next to her while she's sleeping and think about what it would be like to touch her with my hands, which ends up with me doing exactly that and Deb waking up pissed. Sleep is sacred business in our house. Sometimes I think her dream life, that other life of pies and ice cream, is more important than the one she lives with me. But this isn't an askable question. It isn't Englishable.

So I get a beer and then—because I'm sad, because my wife has just turned me out, because tomorrow is Sunday and besides, I-don't-give-a-shit is descending, whatever, anything's enough—I fish the Jim Beam out of the back of the cupboard, ice cubes, pour myself a dose. I don't like to see you like that, Deb says. That's part of the reason she's in bed early on Saturday night. On the other hand, the fact that she's in bed early on a Saturday night and not up late with me, having fun or watching satellite TV, is a big part of why I'm into the Jim Beam right now. It's a vicious circle.

She doesn't like to be looked at because she used to weigh over 300 pounds and I guess over 350 at one point in high school. The pictures from her first wedding are something. It's hard to tell what's the bride and what's the cake.

We don't have a lot of pictures around the house compared to most people. I mean, we've got her sister's kids on the refrigerator, but the big elaborate frames with the ski trips and family Christmases are out. It's like she didn't exist until four or five years ago, like a full-grown, 120-pound baby born out of that 350 pounder. People turn their lives around, it's true. I tell people about what she used to weigh and they just stare at her, just out-and-out stare, looking for evidence of the fat girl. I know why she doesn't like to be looked at.

There isn't any sign, though, not till you touch her. Then you can sometimes feel these little lines or ridges under the surface of her skin, from where it stretched out and then stretched back again, a crazy thing, like the birth of a child. I mean, how could a thing like that happen? The same exact skin that once held three of her. She had a couple of operations, one to get her boobs hitched up again—the ligament or whatever—and then I guess the underside of her chin. But you can't see the scars, you can't see anything, especially not when she's got a tan, which is always. I offered to buy her a tanning bed of her own for Christmas the other year—she's already got a Stairmaster and a Schwinn exercise bike down in the basement. But she said no, she likes going in to the Tanfastic. She doesn't like being cooped up in the house all the time, she says. Which is what? I don't know.

I think about the touch of her skin and I get lonely for her.

Turn on channel 21, the skin channel, and I get even lonelier. What's worse than watching other people fucking? Not even fucking, just pretending. And then the bodies that the girls have, not even touched, not even used. That's one of my theories: people just want to see them get messed up a little, want to see them get used the way the rest of us have been used. I've got a lot of little theories. That's the thing about working with your hands, it gives you more time to think than it gives you things to think about. You realize after a while that the brain isn't always king. For instance, I'm sitting here watching the skin channel because I'm lonely and this is the one thing that makes me even more lonely. I could be watching a documentary on ancient Persia or a midget sprint-car race. For another example, I get up and get another dose of Jim Beam. This particular decision goes like this: I'm fucked anyway so I might as well.

It isn't even two yet.

I don't know how great we're doing.

Debbie didn't lose all that weight just to find me. She lives on fizzy water and carrot sticks and boneless skinless chickens; she suffers. I'd be disappointed if she didn't have hopes and dreams beyond this: a horse, I know she wants a horse, and some new stuff for the living room that doesn't come from Sears this time. That isn't even the start of it, though. There's something driving her. I see her down on the Stairmaster, climbing up to nowhere with a towel around her neck to catch the sweat, and she's got this look on her face. She's not even seeing me. I used to think this was funny—there's a place next to the Winn-Dixie that's got about fifteen of the stair machines in the window next to each other, and you'd see the secretaries and the girls from the community college walking up the ladder to nowhere. We made jokes about wiring those suckers up to run the lights. With Debbie, though, that stairway is going somewhere. She's only twenty-eight. I get another drink to celebrate her success.

I move a porch chair into the middle of the lawn and light a cigar. I'm having all kinds of good ideas.

The chair is the springy-metal kind with the shell back and it makes a noise when I run into the porch rail, and again when I move it out of the harmful radiation of the yard light and into the shadow of the house. That yellow light cannot be good for you. In the dark, though, I can't see the twirls and curves of the cigar smoke, only the red bumblebee of the coal. They say that blind people don't smoke because they don't get the pleasure of seeing it. And out beyond that circle of light is the whole country. One little slip and you could end up in Grand Rapids, Tampa, anywhere—you could just come loose, dislocated. I could, anyway. I didn't grow up here. I've got an ex-wife and a daughter named Tiffany a day's drive away from here. Tell me how I ended up going along with the name Tiffany and you'll have the key. Along with many other things, it's a mystery to me. Like this: Debbie's face when we end up in the girls' section of Penney's or Sears, looking for a birthday treat for my daughter—she gets a hungry look on her face when she walks among all that pink and lace. There's no other word for it: a *hunger*. She *wants* these things. A big pink cake, waiting for her, I see her fingers when she was fat, sneaking frosting when she thought nobody was looking. The hands of really fat people, there's something about them, the way big drooping arms end up in tiny hands.

Somewhere in here I decide that I might just as well just bring the fifth of Jim Beam out onto the lawn with me and I light another cigar besides. What? It's like running a car into a bridge abutment and surviving. Sunday morning is never coming. Debbie's going somewhere. She didn't lose 225 pounds just to find me, I know that much anyway, and the certainty makes me tremble and sweat. All those highways, FM country the same in every town, a McDonald's on every highway corner—it makes me want to throw up. My great-grandfathers would be ashamed of me, and rightly so. You know what pisses me off? Everything pisses me off. What? Every time she passes the refrigerator, she's not eating something. I just think of what's going on in her imagination, in her dreams of T-bone steaks with a half-inch ring of fat, hot off the barbecue, bread and butter and more butter on the corn, moon pies and RC Cola, chopped pork BBQ on a bun, bearclaws and cream horns, pepperoni pizza, all you can eat. I take a drink straight out of the whiskey bottle and I see that I am *living the dream*. The words make me laugh but it's the truth: all the whiskey I can stand to drink, just keep going, follow the thing through: greedy, grasping, like Debbie lost in a supermarket bakery after hours, the pink icing all to herself, living the dream, down on her knees behind the cooler cases of pies and cookies, buttercream braids, French twists, raspberry-swirl cheesecake—I take a drink of Jim Beam straight out of the bottle and I'm laughing hard enough to spill a little down onto my shirt, but it's no big deal, I'm living the dream, there's plenty left to kill me.

Jim, she says. Come to bed. It's time for you to come to bed.

She's out on the lawn in her T-shirt and panties. I could explain to her—living the dream, how we're the same—but then I see that this is not the case. I have been doing something dirty and she has caught me at it.

Sorry, I tell her. The word comes out of my mouth blurry.

You fucker, she says. Put the cigar out and come to bed.

I have been forgiven, I can tell by the way she talks.

I ask her, Come here for a second.

It's bedtime, Jim. It was bedtime a long time ago.

Come here for a second.

I can't see her face in the dark but I know that dirty look.

I have sinned and I have been forgiven and I am suddenly light.

She comes over and sits down in my lap (this is extra, more than I could hope for) and she doesn't weigh anything—this is the flying dream where we don't have any gravity anymore and everything is possible. We look up into the stars and they are spinning in front of our eyes, drunk. Our little story goes forward one more day.

Siobhan Dowd and Jake Kreilkamp—program director and coordinator, respectively, of PEN American Center's Freedom-to-Write Committee—write this column regularly, alerting readers to the plight of writers around the world who deserve our awareness and our writing action.

Writer Detained: William Ojeda Orozco

by Siobhan Dowd

Venezuela for a long time enjoyed a sunnier reputation than many of its Latin American neighbors: while disappearances, military coups, reports of torture and imprisonment dogged the continent, Venezuela, an independent country since 1830, boasted popular elections and relative calm. The last period of political turbulence was in the 1950s when there was a rash of presidents deposed, assassinated, or forced to resign.

Recently, however, Venezuela has been coming under criticism for problems which, despite the rosy image, have been endemic all along. The police force acts with a mind of its own, and has been proven responsible for a recent spate of extra-judicial executions, beatings, and arbitrary arrests, some of them clearly racially motivated (the country's small minority of Native Americans has long been severely discriminated against). Another long-standing problem is that of corruption at all levels of society. Bribery is a way of life. It is employed in small matters and great—to jump queues, or to pervert the course of justice.

It is the latter tendency that, with the imprisonment of William Ojeda Orozco, has attracted international attention. Ojeda, a talented writer and journalist of only twenty-six years, is serving a twelve-month prison sentence for exposing judicial corruption in his first book, *Cuanta Vale un Juez? (How Much is a Judge Worth?)*. A native of Caracas, Ojeda is a staffer for the daily *Ultimas Noticias*, and has worked as a producer for Radio Caracas. Published in 1995, *How Much is a Judge Worth?* quickly became the hot topic of conversation from the Supreme Court down to the slums of Caracas. Most people had no doubt about the book's essential veracity. Even the government official in charge of the justice system, blaming Venezuela's general lack of order, has admitted that corruption is routine. Ojeda's book charted a Byzantine system of gifts, inflated fees, bribes, and favors, incorporating secretaries and Supreme Court Justices, and included a list of judges who, according to him, regularly abuse their position. Ojeda, when pressed, refused to reveal the sources of his information, but swore to its accuracy. The judges exposed said he had merely repeated defamatory hearsay.

The administration of President Rafael Caldera has pledged itself to end corruption, and one of the planks in Caldera's election platform was a promise to create a high commission to re-organize the entire legal system. Even before Ojeda's conviction, the judiciary had become something of a laughingstock. In one instance, a judge, Rosa Natasha Fernandez, was caught with nearly $900 in bribes, hurriedly stuffed into her underpants. When a police officer extracted the bundle of notes from its hiding place in front of forty witnesses, the story made tabloid headlines around the continent. In another case, a judge threw a hail of almost $12,000 in small bills out of her apartment window on hearing that the police were about to undertake a search. The street vendors, passersby, and beggars below had a field day.

Despite this fact, two judges cited in Ojeda's book set about prosecuting him for defamation. Several other judges refused to handle the case, but one was eventually found who declared that Ojeda should be prevented from calling in witnesses in his defense. In November 1996, Ojeda was convicted in absentia to a year in prison. On January 23, however, he gave himself up, but not before delivering the following statement:

> Latin American journalists need to conduct research and investigation in order to strengthen the democratic process in their country, and if I am to be detained as a consequence of publishing the result of my investigations, it is surely a sign that the judiciary is badly in need of real democratic reforms. It is what civil society is urging. As for me, I only performed my duty as a working journalist.

Currently, Ojeda is in El Junquito prison, on Caracas' outskirts. Prison conditions in general in Venezuela are abysmal. According to the New York-based Human Rights Watch, which conducted visits to eleven prisons last year, severe overcrowding leads to a multitude of ills: prisoners sleep in hammocks slung across pipe-access passageways, outbreaks of violence are commonplace, sanitation is non-existent, and in one case, a fire broke out that killed twenty-five inmates.

Ojeda dismisses the prospect of an appeal to the Supreme Court as useless, given that the majority of its justices are implicated in his book. He urges his supporters instead to appeal to President Caldera to grant a pardon, as a first step towards fulfilling the promises he made to secure his election.

Please send appeals for Ojeda's release to:

His Excellency Dr. Rafael Caldera
President of the Republic of Venezuela
Palacio Miraflores
Caracas, Venezuela

Carolyn Kizer

CAROLYN KIZER

Poet

Interview

by Jim Schumock

Photo credit Chris Felver

Carolyn Kizer

Pulitzer Prize-winning poet Carolyn Kizer was born in Spokane, Washington in 1925. She has published numerous collections, including* Knock Upon Silence, Mermaids in the Basement, YIN, The Nearness of You, The Ungrateful Garden, *and* Midnight Was My Cry. *She is also the author of* Proses: Essays on Poets and Poetry. *Founder of Poetry Northwest, her current collection,* Harping On: Poems, 1985-1995, *was published by Copper Canyon Press.

SCHUMOCK: *Was Spokane a provincial backwater for you? Or was it as useful a place as any for a young poet?*

KIZER: Well, it certainly was a provincial backwater. I think almost every good poet I know came from another provincial backwater, usually in the Midwest. In other words, I think part of what prompted us to write poetry was the need to entertain ourselves because we were bored silly. No inland city, no matter

Glimmer Train Stories, Issue 24, Fall 1997

of what size, has the degree of sophistication of even a small town on the ocean or on a major river. There's something about the international intercourse and the flow of people to and from other countries. It gives a sophistication that no inland city has. Spokane was, and is, extremely provincial. I have a friend there named James McAuley who runs the Eastern Washington University Press. He always introduces me by quoting a line from a poem of mine called "Running Away from Home," which is, "After Spokane, what horrors lurk in Hell?" Then, he smiles like a cat and waits for the audience to react.

I know you've traveled widely and lived in a lot of different places. Is there any place you feel as at home as you did in Spokane?

Oh, I feel much more at home anywhere from Vancouver, British Columbia to San Francisco. That's my area, provided it sticks pretty close to the coast. I'm always just delighted to be in Port Townsend or Vancouver or Victoria or the Oregon Coast, which I dote on. I love San Francisco. I love where I live in Sonoma, which is about fifty miles north. I feel a kind of regional identity far more than I do to a specific city.

As an only child of parents who were already in late middle age at your birth, were you spoiled by them?

I don't know quite what spoiled means, really. The advantages were enormous, of course, because young parents go out a lot. They go out dancing and they go to parties. But middle-aged and older parents tend to stay home with their kids. My father read aloud to me every night or my mother did. I certainly had much too much attention. I can't really regret it because I think it helped make a poet out of me.

Your father was an attorney, and a number of your poems have to do with him. Are you still dealing with your relationship with him?

I think one does forever. I really do. My relationship with my father was far more ambiguous than that with my mother. My mother was a very high-strung and an extremely neurotic person. I was crazy about her. She was lots of fun. They were both wonderful storytellers but Mother, in particular, was a magnificent storyteller. She certainly put her fingers in my innards in ways that made me very uncomfortable as an adolescent, but I loved her very dearly. I always found her amusing. Daddy was a little more difficult. He had never been around a child. He didn't know what a child needed or wanted, particularly a girl child. I think it was very hard for him at fifty to have this little creature. You probably know that from my book, *The Nearness of You.* I've got a poem called "Thrall" about my relations with my father when I was little. They were difficult. They went on being difficult. He was absolutely devoted to me. I suppose I loved him, but I didn't love him as much as I loved my mother.

He was, as your mother was, very active politically in a lot of different organizations. People from around the world came to your house, too.

Yes, they did. Along with Roger Baldwin, Daddy founded the American Civil Liberties Union. Daddy was instrumental in the planning movement in this country. Although, tragically, it went into decline at the time of the war. War is always used as an excuse to crush anything progressive that happens to be around. God knows, he tried. He was very active in things like the United Nations Association. He was a real internationalist. When he was picked to run the United Nations Relief Program in China during and after World War II, he had that extraordinary experience of living and working in Chung-king. In many ways, I don't think he was particularly suited for it. I don't think he was an administrator. I don't think he was a particularly good judge of character. My mother would have been far better. I can remember parties in Shanghai when we were surrounded by international sharks. Really, people went there with the basest of motives. It was either to get rich quick or to escape from a lurid past. Daddy was oblivious to most of them. My mother picked up on them immediately. She could spot a phony at twenty paces. So, his China experience was a very mixed one. He was very popular with the staff because he was an absolutely upright person in an almost entirely corrupt atmosphere.

What do you think he would have done if he hadn't been an attorney?

His own version of that was when he was a young man and his family came to Spokane and his father went bankrupt, one of the ways that he made money was to read aloud to elderly Southern lawyers who were fugitives from Reconstruction. They were men of high learning with great collections of books. Daddy saw all these wonderful leather-bound copies with gold printing on the backs. If you were a lawyer you could have books! That's what he really wanted. Oh, I think planning really was the love of his life. Of course, he had a large civil-liberties practice during World War I. A man named Kizer was at a certain disadvantage for obvious reasons. He defended and tried to protect the Germans in the community from hate. He was a thoroughly fine and good person in every way. A noble person. But fatherhood wasn't really one of his major talents, I have to say.

I know one of the people he caused to come to your house and spend a fair amount of time in Spokane was Vachel Lindsay.

Oh, yes. Vachel ran an ad in a newspaper. I think it must have been the *New York Times*. He was asking, in his rather florid manner, if anyone would like to exchange poems for bread.

I love that.

Yeah, bread. When that term became in use by hippies in the '70s, it really took me back. So, my father immediately wrote and said, "Yes, I would." He sent him a railroad ticket. Vachel came out and landed on us. Daddy made an agreement with Mr. Davenport of the Davenport Hotel, which was then justly famous, to put up Vachel. Daddy paid most of the rent and Mr. Davenport forgot the rest. Vachel was around for several years. He was a rather difficult guest, in many ways. He had a large, braying laugh that used to set my mother's teeth on edge. He was not an attractive personality. He had an almost fatal insularity at a time when James Joyce and the French Surrealists and Eliot and

Ezra Pound, all these people, were fomenting new movements. He resolutely turned his back on this. He was really a prairie provincial much in the way of Carl Sandburg. His work suffers severely because of that.

Your mother was, at one point, a Wobbly organizer. I think that's fascinating! She also had a Ph.D. from Stanford?

Yes, she was a biologist. She was the head of the department at Mills and at San Francisco State. That was pretty unusual for a woman of her generation to be active in that particular line of work. I think she should have been a psychiatrist, actually. She would have been terrific because she was so extraordinarily intuitive. Of course, being highly neurotic herself she was good at dealing with other neurotics, including me.

She had some other interests and occupations as well along the way, didn't she?

Oh, yes. She painted. She painted rather well. We had a big studio in our house. Among other things, she started the WPA Art Center in Spokane. She did it in a rather unusual way. She collected quarters and dimes and dollars from cab drivers, from hair dressers, and gasoline-station attendants. When we finally got the art center—of course, she had some big donors, too—but when we finally got the art center built these people felt that they were part of it. Now, in Seattle, Mrs. Fuller and her son, Richard, put up all the money for the Seattle Art Museum, which stood high on a hill in a rather pretentious building. Ordinary people would not go. They thought it was not for them. But our art center was right in the middle of downtown and everybody went, including me at the age of twelve. I studied painting with wonderful painters. One of them was Carl Morris and his sculptor girlfriend, Hilda Grossman. He later married her and came over here and became an eminent artist in Portland. Another one was Guy Anderson, who celebrated his ninetieth birthday with a one-man show at the Seattle Art Museum the other day. That was wonderful for a young girl to have that kind of exposure to art. The other people in my classes at the art center were just ordinary kids because they felt that they had an investment in it. That was part of my mother's genius.

Beyond being read to aloud by both of your parents, you were early influenced by writings like Arthur Waley's translations from the Chinese.

My mother read Waley to me and she read Robinson Jeffers and Whitman. Daddy read me Keats and then he read more Keats and then he read still more Keats.

Who were some of the first people that you read on your own?

I read very early and I was read to very early. I've always said that if Daddy had read me Keats' letters instead of his poems, which were beyond me, it would have made a big difference. The letters are magnificent. I think any young person would appreciate them. I remember coming home very angry—I think I was about eleven—and saying to my parents indignantly, "Why didn't you ever read me Dryden and Pope?" They fell back, stunned. I had discovered Pope, the great satirist and wit. That was my cup of tea far more than Keats. Then, of course, later I discovered the Roman satirists. These people were very, very important to me. Still are. I admired Browning very much because I felt that his was my line of country—the exploration of character and the nuances of character and what happens when one person meets and influences another person. But his rhymes were so relentless that I was afraid of getting them into my head. Shakespeare, of course, was the great purifier of the language of the tribe. It has always baffled me why the English, who had all these great poets behind them—all the great seventeenth-century metaphysicals and Shakespeare and Pope and so on—fell into this terrible mechanical stressing. It ruined a lot of good poets. I'm trying to think who influenced me absolutely on my own. I don't think anybody did. I think, with the exception of Pope and Dryden, my parents got there first. But they had far more conventional taste than I did. I had to find people like Eliot and Stevens and Pound on my own.

Eventually, you went away to Sarah Lawrence College, but you credit Theodore Roethke at the University of Washington with really bringing you alive to the writing of poetry.

Oh, yes. The writing staff at Sarah Lawrence was very ordinary, really. There was an early politically radical feminist named Genevieve Taggart who was my professor. First, there was a man named Horace Gregory. I was very much under the influence of Robert Frost then. World War II had just begun. I had written a poem about a farm woman whose child had been lost at sea. She took the basket that she had woven as his cradle out in the backyard and buried it. You can see the Frost all over that! Well, Horace Gregory looked at this poem. It described farm animals. He said, "You have pigs in this poem; *pigs are not poetic.*" I got up and walked out of the class and never went back. Anyway, then I fell under the sway of Ms. Taggart. She would lie back on her chaise lounge in a cloud of "perfume and musk and intellectual blackmail," as I said in a poem called "Pro Feminina." She would say, "Darling, this is a wonderful poem, send it to the *New Yorker*," or she'd say, "Darling, this poem isn't very good." She'd drop it in the waste basket. She didn't have a clue about how you made a good poem out of a bad poem, which is the thing Roethke taught me. That's the answer to it all, really.

What is the answer?

My first drafts are still terrible, by and large. I really don't want people to see most of them. It's learning how to have a sense of detachment about your work and look at it as you would look at somebody else's and fix it up. You have to be ruthless. You remember that wonderful thing Samuel Johnson said. I always hate to quote Johnson because if you don't do it exactly right the cadences don't fall correctly. Johnson said, "On reading something you have written, if you come across a passage that seems to you extraordinarily fine, cut it out." That's so true most of the time. Ted Roethke said, "Any fool can take a bad line out of a poem; it takes a real pro to throw out a good line." Sometimes good lines are not adding anything to a poem. You have them in there because you're enjoying your own skills but it doesn't relate to the overall theme or the dramatic structure of the poem. Throw it out. You always save those so you can use them somewhere else. They act sort of like starters when you're making bread. But then, you wrap them around another poem and eventually you throw them out of that poem, too. It's sort of like the cannibalization of automobiles. We cannibalize a lot of poetry, too.

I remember reading, and being altered by, the collection Five Northwest Poets. *It included you, Kenneth O. Hanson, William Stafford, David Wagoner, and Richard Hugo. That was really a signal book. It said the Northwest is fertile literary ground. What did that collection mean for you?*

Of course, I was terribly pleased to be in it as the only woman. I think the thing that has stayed with me over the years is the extraordinary introduction that Robin Skelton, the English poet transplanted to Victoria, British Columbia wrote, because Skelton was so prescient. We were all young poets then. Bill Stafford was a little older. But Skelton saw our potential in an extraordinary way. When I reread it now, I'm stunned at how closely observant he was. The book is very scarce. You never see it in secondhand bookstores. Most people who have owned it have had it pinched, including me. So, it occurred to me that it would be nice to bring out a memorial edition of it now that Dick Hugo is dead and Bill Stafford is dead. Kenneth Hanson lives permanently in Greece. Only David Wagoner and I alone are here to tell you. I think it would be really nice to do a deluxe edition of it with the Carl Morris illustrations. I hope we can do that sometime while Dave and I are still around. There was a very funny occasion when the five of us gave a reading here in Portland. The book was dedicated to Roethke, who had just died. All five of us got up and read. We all paid a tribute to Roethke of one kind or another because he had meant a great deal to all of us. Bill Stafford, in his own inimitable way, said, "Never read Roethke much, wasn't influenced by him, didn't like his work, etc." Dick Hugo then got up and said, "Thank you, Martin Bormann!" There was that wonderful iconoclastic independence of Bill Stafford that was one of his great virtues, I think. He was no man's follower, slave, whatever.

Do you think there was a validation of the Northwest as being a literary place?

No, I think it was a validation of Roethke. I think that any university, anywhere, if it hires one or two men and women who are absolutely tops, they will collect the best people around. I mean Dave came from Indiana. Bill came from Kansas, despite his denials. Ken came from Drain, Oregon—poor thing. Of course, I'm from Spokane. Roethke made me a poet. There's no question of it. I think any school, anywhere, today can build a reputation with an amazingly few number of people. People generally think of Berkeley. They've got dozens of brilliant people and Nobel winners and so on. It doesn't take that many.

In fact, that might obscure the whole thing.

Yes, I think you could make a good argument for that.

You know, there's a line that your father said: "The last thing we learn about ourselves is our effect."

That's very true, don't you think?

Yes, I do. Could you expand on that a little bit? What it meant for him? Or for you in poetry?

Well, I can't even remember the context now. I know that I was immensely impressed when he said this in his nineties. He had had some kind of revelation about his effect on people, or perhaps I had, and we were discussing it. He came out with this. I thought, and I still think, it's incredibly true. Every once in a while somebody will say to me, "Oh, you're so formidable." Or, "When I first met you, I was frightened of you." I'm always stunned by this. Is it because I'm five feet, ten and a half in my bare feet? I don't feel formidable. Yet, I know there are people who find me so. I think that goes for a lot of other qualities as well. It is very hard to know one's self. We have to, I think, in some degree, depend upon querying other people about what we're like. We can't depend on our own judgment. I always like to quote from *Troilus and Cressida*: "I am mine own woman, well at ease." I think if you have a certain kind of self-confidence, which I owe entirely to my parents, some people can find that rather threatening.

When Richard Hugo was asked what made poets different from other people he said, "Poets think about death all the time*!"*

Yes, he did say that.

Do you?

Oh, yes. But as I get older it bothers me far less. I remember one time—I think I was in my late twenties—I had had three children in three years and I was kind of tired. I was not happily married. I said to my mother, "Mama, at what age did you feel oldest?" She thought about it for a while and she said, "Twenty-eight." I think that's a great truth. When you get to be really old, you reach a kind of accommodation and you don't think about it nearly as much. I think when we're young and when we're writing, one of the ways we fend off the notion of our mortality is with putting words down on a piece of paper.

What about alcohol? That's a way to fend off mortality. For your generation, it was really a major catalyst.

Of course, Dick Hugo and James Wright were alcoholics. But look at the previous batch. Lowell and so on. They were not only alcoholics, they were all crazy. I think all poets, with the exception of William Stafford, tend to drink. I remember the first time I was at a conference where several of us were giving readings, and someone asked Bill if he'd like a preliminary drink, and he said, "Oh, I never drink before a reading." We all just sort of looked at him. Yes, we do drink. That's very true.

Why?

Oh, I think it takes the edge off things a bit. I think most poets are rather shy. We can come on awfully strong but it doesn't mean a whole lot. We're all rather reticent. We're very vulnerable. A couple of drinks makes us a little more socially comfortable.

There's a line you wrote about the idea of growing old alive and about staying vivid as you age. I look in your eyes and I've looked at your picture on your books jackets and your eyes are still the eyes of a young girl.

That's very nice. It's probably because I'm nearsighted. Nearsighted people have good eyes, generally.

I don't think so. I think it's because you've worked hard at staying vivid.

Oh, I don't know about that. I just think one works hard at responding to things and not becoming dull—dulled to sensation, that is. The important thing is never to take anything for granted. Never to find oneself mouthing clichés, or feeling clichés—which is worse. Of course, part of it is genetic, part of it is a question of temperament. All these things enter in. There are no single answers to anything.

I imagine your parents were not dullards.

The interesting thing is that they were both such enormously vivid personalities and such strong personalities. It's a wonder that I wasn't just a little brown bird instead of this road-company Valkyrie, as I once characterized myself.

Literarily speaking, who currently buoys you up with their writing and their insights? Who do you read to lift yourself up?

I know I'll leave out somebody terribly important and hurt their feelings. There are lots of people I like. I think the real test is whose books do you get without reading the reviews. Automatically, I get Adrienne Rich, Denise Levertov, who now lives in Seattle which is good for us all, Phil Levine down in California, W.S. Merwin in Hawaii. There are lots more but that's a rough account. The people I've named are all people of my own generation. Of course, there are lots of younger people coming along like Li-Young Lee, who's just remarkable, I think.

Yes. And Arthur Sze who's in Tucson. They're both Chinese-Americans. And Sherman Alexie who's American-Indian, from my home, Spokane. It's a little frightening, because you don't want to leave out people who are important to you, but I try to read as much as I can. Of course, I'm now at an age where I see certain kinds of poetry—like language poetry, which leaves me somewhat appalled, because when you throw out syntax you've thrown out the skeleton and you're left with a pile of flesh.

You give Philip Levine a lot of credit, justly so, for writing for the working man.

Yes, I do. I love poems about work. There aren't enough of them. I love Gary Snyder very, very much, because Gary is dealing with the natural world in a way that I can relate to, although I'm not an outdoorsy person at all, really. If I take a walk in the woods, I want it to be on a well-trodden path. I love, too, another one of my contemporaries, Robert Creeley. Bob has such an extraordinary command of language. He's unique. No one is like him.

Galway Kinnell does a great job with the working man, as well.

Well, Galway, I suppose, is our truest inheritor of the Whitman tradition. Thank goodness we have one or two who are. That's very, very important. I'm always saying you cannot be an American poet unless you know Whitman. That goes for Dickinson, as well. I think I'd now add Wallace Stevens, although you never come to the end of Wallace Stevens. There are always more things to learn every time you read him. We are fortunate today that we have so many good poets. So many of them are women. I'm very pleased about that. It's very gratifying to me that women have come into their own. I have a collection that you haven't mentioned. I'll put in a little plug here. It's called *100 Great Poems by Women*. It's edited by me with an introduction, and published by Ecco Press. It was really quite extraordinary to put this collection together. I was appalled how few women there were in standard anthologies. I knew these men [the anthologizers] were not male chauvinists. Where were the women? So, you go back and you dig around and you look hard. You find out that the women who were writing up until almost the time of Elizabeth Barrett Browning were members of the nobility—duchesses, countesses. Actually, it begins after Anonymous, with Queens: Elizabeth and Mary. Women commonly had twenty children in those days—many of them died at birth or in early childhood. So, it was only women who had certain comforts in life and had servants to look after the children who had any time to write at all. As it worked out, I found five women per century. That's not very many. Later, they were all spinsters—right up to Marianne Moore. Every successful woman writer was single. That tells you something. As I say in one of my favorite sentences of my own, "Plumbing, birth control, and the vote made it possible for woman to write."

So, the pram in the hallway mitigated against women as well as men.

Oh, did it mitigate against men? You could have fooled me.

What's behind the title of your current collection?

All the meanings of harpist, harpy, and someone who is a common scold, like me. There's a poem in it that I wrote about the Gulf War. I was in Portland giving a reading at Powell's. The Gulf War had broken out and I was very, very depressed and upset about it. My campus then, which was the University of California at Davis, after a great outburst of student protest, suddenly had yellow ribbons all over the place. The students had all been converted to the war. As the train left Portland and wound through Eugene, I looked out and saw a porch where someone had hung an enormous black flag. I wanted to get off the train and hug him. I write a villanelle every few years. It's always on a line from another writer that has struck me. This one has a line from the great French poet, Paul Valery: "The whole green sky is dying, The last tree flares." It's a dark poem, I'm afraid.

There's nothing really light about war.

No.

With all your travels and all the places that you've lived, has the Northwest remained important to you as a psychic grounding?

Oh, I think so. Yes. I certainly don't write out of any other environment. We have lived in Paris part time for five or six years. We've lived in Sonoma for almost ten years now. Neither of those environments have entered my work at all. There's the poem to my husband in which I mentioned California when I say, "Happy people are monogamous, even in California." That's about as close as I get.

What about the despoiling of the rivers and the forests and the changes in the Northwest you've seen over your lifetime?

Oh, it just destroys me. Gary Snyder asked me to participate in a series that he was having at Davis on nature. I said, "Gary, what's happened to my country? It's so tragic to me I can't even think about it, let alone write about it." He said, "Come up and talk about that." I did. I wrote a poem, a long poem. It's about the cutting down of the forests in the Northwest, specifically about Mount Index. I want to warn you if you have a word processor and you want to call a poem "Index" you're in trouble, because the word processor will not accept it! An index is an index is an index, it is not a mountain. Anyway, I wrote about what it was like to grow up in this absolutely glorious Northwest of ours and see it systematically despoiled. It's still going on. It's very upsetting to me. I think imagination failed and is still failing. Of course, the people controlling our lives—the large corporations—they're heartless and soulless and they don't care. Until we can take back our country from these people, I have very little hope for us.

One of your poems, A Muse of Water, *shows us that even in the best of times, when the earth has a lot resources to heal itself, we're still on the edge of oblivion.*

I think I really owe that poem to my father and his passion for planning. I think it's probably the poem that he's influenced more than any other. It's also one of my first feminist poems, because I do intimate strongly that we're in the state that we're in because of men. It's a play on "O, for a Muse of Fire." I'll tell you the genesis of that. The poet, Robert Lowell, was visiting in Seattle. He delivered himself of his belief that women, in the traditional German phrase, should stick to church, kitchen, and children. I was so outraged. I went home and wrote a sizzling invective directed at Lowell. It turned into this poem. As I was rereading the poem to myself, I said, "Lowell doesn't deserve this poem." I took out all the references to him that I could think of. One snuck in and stayed in and that's the reference to the Charles River in Boston. Like a vermiform appendix, it's still hanging around in that poem. That's how it all began. I was really in a white-hot fury. There were two or three other women writers in the room and I thought it was a most tactless act. But then, of course, he was quite mad at the time.

Speaking of rivers, if you were abandoned alone for the rest of your life on a little island in the middle of the Spokane River and you could only take along two books and one piece of music, which ones would you take, Carolyn?

I would take *The Marriage of Figaro* for the music. Can I have the whole opera?

Certainly.

Oh, good. And I would take *The Letters of Gustave Flaubert and George Sand* for one of the books, and then, I guess, I'd have to take the Bible.

What if that were already there as a literary reference and I gave you another book?

The reason the Bible is so important to me is the Psalms. I think the rhythm of the Psalms have really entered into my work a lot.

It's really important to me. I can't have an anthology, I don't suppose?

Yes, you can have an anthology, even a collected works.

All right: a collection of seventeenth-century metaphysical poets with George Herbert, John Donne—all those great guys.

Jim Schumock interviews authors-on-tour for literary radio programs in Portland, Oregon. He is a major contributor to "Between the Covers" on KBOO and "Spotlight on Authors" on KBPS. A collection of his interviews, *Conversations with American Authors*, will be published this fall by Black Heron Press of Seattle, Washington.

Nomi Eve

Here I am, three years old, already digging into my grandfather's orchard. Avichail, Israel, 1971.

Nomi Eve's stories have been published in the *Village Voice Literary Supplement* and *International Quarterly*. She has an MFA in fiction writing from Brown University, and has worked as a freelance book reviewer for the *Village Voice*, the *Boston Globe*, *New York Newsday*, the *Jerusalem Post*, and *Publisher's Weekly*. She was recently awarded the Crossing Boundaries Award for Innovative Fiction by *International Quarterly*.

Eve is currently living in Boston.

Nomi Eve

To Conjure the Twin

My father has researched our family history all the way back to the seventeenth century. What I am doing is juxtaposing his written family history with my own fiction. Everything my father has written is true. Everything I write is what I imagine.

My father writes:

My father, Peretz, and his twin brother, Ishai, were absolutely identical. Most people had trouble telling them apart. There are many stories in our family about how one was always being confused for the other. In 1948, during the Israeli War of Independence, my uncle Ishai was commanding his unit on the outskirts of Petach Tikvah. On the seventeenth of Tamuz, 1948, we lost Ishai. My father felt the bullet enter his twin's back. I was just a little boy, but I remember that day well. My father had been out in the orchard when he came inside with my mother, hunched over, complaining of a terrible pain.

I write:

Peretz could feel it. His skin was neither broken nor bleeding, but the wound was definitely there. Reaching his right hand up over his left shoulder, he tried to press out the hurt. As if maybe it were just a kink in the muscle or a momentary disalignment of the bone. But the wound would not go away; rather, as he pressed, it worsened, until it stabbed and burned and blasted all through him. Falling to his knees, Peretz let his hand come back around and slide onto the ground by his hip. Then he began to sob. Because the wound in his shoulder had neither logical source nor palpable manifestation.

After lying on the ground for several minutes, Peretz sat up, got to his feet, and moved towards the house. He advanced in a lopsided shuffle, his right arm flung once more over his left shoulder, the palm of his hand pressing into the epicenter of the pain. "Ishai has been shot!" he yelled to Rifka, as he emerged from the trees. Rifka, who was behind the house at the wash basin, said nothing in response, but led her husband up the back-porch stairs and into the little bedroom, and then ran for the doctor. The doctor did not find anything wrong with the shoulder. He told Peretz, with calm voice and caring eyes, that no man can feel another's pain, and that, "Although there is no superficial evidence to suggest a problem, perhaps an internal muscle had been torn or strained somewhere below the skin as a result of heavy manual labor." The doctor insisted that all would be better in a few days.

Rifka, sitting by the bed, stared at the floor. She did not see the doctor out. And when, just an hour later, Lazzie Friedman walked up the front path and into the house with the news of Ishai's death, Rifka found herself listening not to the man in front of her, but to the messenger she could not see, that invisible invader who had been sent by some mad god or all-too-sane devil to hold horrible conversation with the muscular curve in the left side of her husband's back. Rifka reached out and held Peretz's head into her waist, her hands on his shoulders.

Lazzie told them that Ishai had died immediately. And that the bullet that killed him had entered just under the left clavicle. And that his body was safe in the bunker. And that he was a hero whom they all had loved. Lazzie cried as he spoke. Holding Peretz's sob-wracked body, Rifka wailed too.

When the doctor and Lazzie Friedman left the house, Peretz got out of bed. He ran through the house, and out into the orchard where he retched onto a patch of knotty ground. His heaves were empty and painful. When the nausea passed, he looked up into the boughs and then back towards the house and thought: This is one death that will not be easily buried.

And Peretz was right. Ishai's funeral would be held the following day in the city of Petach Tikvah, the city whose name means "the Opening of Hope." But the twin's death would not suffer earth to be laid upon it. A kind of phantom twinship remained adamantly above ground in Peretz's keeping for over fifty years. Ishai's death was like some queer fruit that neither ripened nor fell, but remained pendent in stagnant unnatural grace on the tree.

My father writes:

On the day that he was killed, Ishai had been planning to leave his unit for an hour and have lunch with his parents in Petach Tikva. After he was informed of Ishai's death, Peretz immediately got out of bed and went to his parents' house to tell them the awful news. When he arrived, he walked up the front steps. His mother, Gila, who was waiting for Ishai to come to lunch, saw Peretz through the screen door. She thought it was Ishai. "Ishai, come in, Ishai," she said. Peretz, her other son, fainted. Later he told me, "Ishai was gone, and my mother thought that I was Ishai. It was just too much."

I write:

Gila opened the door and fell on top of her son who had fallen. When she landed, she found her face pressing into her son's chest and her knees twisted to the left of his hip. Her hands, which she had thrown out to break her fall, were firmly palming either side of his head. All in all it was not an awful fall. Just a strange one. She was never quite nimble and was used to tripping and banging herself about. But this was the first time that she had ever fallen on top of one of her sons.

The strangest thing about the fall was, of course, that her son, whom she thought Ishai, had fallen in the first place.

"Ishai," she said nervously, "Ishai, wake up." But he didn't wake up. Gila repeated, this time yelling, "Ishai, wake up!" That was when she saw the subtle indentations on the side of Peretz's head. The indentations, tiny, almost unnoticeable, were really just flat spots no bigger than if a pinkie finger had pressed there and left a mark. Peretz's name meant "to burst." She had named him after the first of a pair of biblical twins to emerge from their mother's womb. But unlike his biblical namesake, her Peretz had not quite burst out of the womb. The doctor had pulled him out of her with a pair of forceps. She, a new young mother, had first cursed and cried over those marring spots, but then, rather quickly, she grew to appreciate them, for the mechanical markings (which were really so small that no one but a mother would notice them) provided her with a sure tool of telling which boy was which. For while her boys were always tricking the rest of the world, all she ever had to do was look on the side of their heads. Ishai, the second twin born, had slid easily out of her body after his brother, and so his brow had stayed smooth.

Gila did not move. And Peretz's chest pounded up and down underneath her. His was no faint of delicate repose, but seemed a kind of eyes-closed struggle. It was a hot day and sweat covered both of their bodies. The mother reached her hands to the side of the son's head and touched lightly on the spots that made him different from the one whom she had expected.

When Michel came out of the orchard and round to the front of the house, and saw his wife lying almost astride their son, he did not know what to think. He started to yell, "What are you doing? What are you doing?" It was such an odd, disturbing sight. He started to run towards them, but was not in time to stop Gila from pressing hard on the sides of Peretz's head. She was pressing not to cause her son pain, but to make those tiny forceps spots disappear. No, of course this didn't make sense. One cannot just press and poke and refashion a skull. And if one could, to press would only make the spots deeper. But Gila was not thinking of all this. Her logic consisted of the desperate, panicked need to conjure the twin named Ishai out of the twin named Peretz between her palms. For she may have been a clumsy woman, but she was also a very smart one. She had easily deciphered the code: the forceps spots coupled with the faint, and with the fact that Ishai was a commander in a war written like all wars with the blood ink of so many beloved dead and wounded, equaled the death of Ishai and the announcing presence of the unconscious Peretz in his place.

Of course, her pressing caused pain. And the son awoke with it, just as his father reached the front door, and bent down to push Gila's hands off of Peretz's forehead.

All three huddled together on the front path, screaming and thrashing and sick with grief.

Ann Hood

This is the photo that my kids picked for me to send. They liked the hat and the funny smile. I'm three years old and dressed in what must have been my favorite outfit: I'm wearing it in all the pictures taken of me from 1960.

Ann Hood is the author of six novels, including *Somewhere Off the Coast of Maine*, *Places to Stay the Night*, and *The Properties of Water*, which was published in paperback by Bantam Books in 1995. She lives in Providence, Rhode Island with her husband and their three children. Before becoming a full-time writer, she was a TWA flight attendant. The story "Dropping Bombs" had its genesis in conversations and experiences she shared with many of her gay friends there. It's a story about love and acceptance, one she has tried to get right for a long time.

Ann Hood

Dropping Bombs

Jim told his mother everything. He explained every detail, every reason, every step. How Aunt Dodie could drive her to the airport and wait with her while she picked up her ticket. How to pack in a small bag that she could take on the plane with her so she wouldn't have to worry about her things getting lost. How once she boarded, she did not have to worry about anything at all because the pilot would do the rest. "Once you take off," he told her, "just sit back and relax." He even sent her some paperbacks and a stack of cooking magazines to read en route. "You'll be in Los Angeles in time for lunch," he said.

But still she couldn't handle it. With increased airport security he couldn't meet her at the gate, so Jim told her to wait for him at baggage claim. "But you said not to check a bag," Eve said, and Jim could hear the shrill panic rising in her voice. "Just follow the signs to baggage claim. Hell," he told her, "follow all the other passengers. Then just stand there. I'll find you." Instead, she stood at the gate, frozen there in her new mauve pantsuit, clutching her bag to her chest, eyes wild like a trapped animal.

Jim got to the airport almost an hour early and stood watching each new planeload of passengers arrive and claim their bags. Even after everyone left, the luggage carousels kept spinning, sending a few unclaimed bags around again and again. Jim kept

Glimmer Train Stories, Issue 24, Fall 1997

wondering who owned those bags. Wasn't that unsafe? Couldn't some crazed terrorist check a bag with a bomb in it and then not board the flight at all? Those bags worried him, circling endlessly like that.

A redcap passed him.

"Excuse me," Jim said, and he pointed toward Carousel C. The same two bags had been going around on it since Jim arrived, a small brown leather one that looked like a mail pouch and a beat-up, dusty blue duffel bag.

The red cap looked at Jim like he didn't trust him. The whites of his eyes were yellow. They reminded Jim of eggs.

"Those bags," Jim said, wagging his finger, "whose are they?"

Slowly, the man turned and studied the circling luggage. "Well," he said, "how am I supposed to know that now?" He pointed too, at Carousel B, where a fresh group of passengers jockeyed for position. "Whose bags are those?" he said, and he wagged his finger at the luggage cluttering the carousel. "You think I go around, matching up bags with people?"

The man wore his hat far back on his head, revealing a short, military-type haircut. For an instant, Jim pictured him fighting a war, in Korea maybe, rushing forward, angry and mean.

"You think I got nothing better to do?" the man was saying.

"It just seems dangerous," Jim said. "That's all." He was aware that he was still half-pointing, his wrist drooping slightly, his finger pointing downward.

"Yeah," the red cap said. "Them bags are real dangerous. You keep your eye on them."

He lifted his empty cart, aiming toward Carousel B, where passengers were claiming their luggage now in a frenzy that reminded Jim of animals gobbling their prey on National Geographic specials.

A loudspeaker crackled and a voice announced, "James Morgan, please meet your mother at the TWA ticket counter, upper level."

"Shit," Jim said, startled to hear his own name like that.

The red cap had started to move away from him. As he wheeled past Jim he muttered, "Faggot."

"I can't believe you didn't come for me. I waited just like you said. I waited and waited. Finally this nice girl, maybe a stewardess, I don't know, she came up to me and said, 'Are you lost?' and I told her my son was supposed to be there. That he was late or forgot or something." Eve glared at him. "I waited forever, just like you said."

They were at an outdoor restaurant in Venice, eating lunch. His mother had told Jim the story twice already, first when he claimed her and then again in the car on their way here. She also told him it was impossible to read on the flight. "You have to stay alert," she said. "Anyone could be a hijacker. A Shiite Moslem or Libyan terrorist. Who knows? Do you think Klinghoffer, cruising like that on the Mediterranean, expected to be shot and dumped in the sea? You don't know who to trust." She'd handed him the paperbacks and cooking magazines, still in the padded shipping envelope he'd sent them in.

Now Jim pointed toward the parade of people that whizzed past them on roller blades, bicycles, skateboards, and roller skates. "Look at them," he told his mother. "See how everyone looks different out here."

She snorted. "So I noticed," she said. "Too many of them dye their hair. And they spend too much time in the sun. Don't they read out here? It's very dangerous." She sipped her iced tea and made a face. "This is terrible."

"I mean they're more active," Jim said. "Health conscious. Any day of the week you'll see people out here like this."

"Great," Eve said. "Wonderful." She looked around until she spotted their waiter, then motioned him over. "What is in this tea?" she said to him.

He was handsome, tanned and blond with a dimple in his chin. He looked first at Jim and smiled, then at Eve. "Fresh mint," he said. "Isn't it yummy?"

"If I wanted mint," she said, "I'd chew gum."

The waiter looked at Jim again. Jim felt a warm familiar rush in his gut. Sometimes he wondered if the real reason he had moved to L.A. was because he liked these surfer boys so much. He imagined for an instant this waiter naked, no tan lines, a smooth hairless chest.

"Could I just have some water?" Eve was saying.

"You bet," the waiter said, smiling again. When he left, he brushed against Jim, so lightly it felt the breeze from the water that lay ahead of them.

Eve studied Jim's face, hard.

"What?" he said.

She shook her head.

Jim cleared his throat and looked off toward the ocean. He had lived in L.A. for almost three years and this was the first time his mother had come to visit. He'd asked her in the past, tried to lure her here with promised trips to Mann's Chinese Theatre and Disneyland, places that she'd always heard about and thought she'd never see. Secretly, he was always relieved when she refused to come. She would say, "I'll see you out here at Christmas anyway. Right?" And he would feel a ballooning in his chest, a fullness that he liked. He would think, Good. It was like buying a few more months of not having to tell her.

Once, she'd said yes, then canceled at the last minute. "There are some things I really don't want to see," she'd said as way of an explanation. That had startled Jim. What exactly had that meant? Even now he wondered if she was trying to tell him something, if maybe she knew somehow already. But that seemed impossible. When he'd lived in Chicago, just an hour from her house in the suburbs, he was still pretending, even to himself. He used to date girls who were pretty, former Homecoming queens, girls who dressed in pale colors, who wore soft fuzzy sweaters and pink lipstick. Last Christmas he noticed that his mother still had a picture of him with one of those girls, one she especially liked named Debbie, right on top of the television set. In it, Jim is slightly behind Debbie, so that it is her smiling, heart-shaped face that dominates. It is her locket, her wispy blond bangs and bright pink lips that you noticed. Jim was really in the background, a blur.

"Jim?" his mother said. She reached across the table and squeezed his hand. "Jim," she said again, "how are you? Are you happy?"

He had decided that if she really came this time, he would tell her. But now he wasn't so sure. She did not seem ready. Why, even a glass of tea with mint in it threw her into a tizzy! Even the sight of healthy, tanned people upset her! Sometimes, when he was alone, her face floated in front of him, frowning and disappointed, holding all the pain of knowing the truth, of knowing there would never be a big church wedding at Our Lady of Perpetual Sorrow, or grandchildren, or even him at home for Christmas with his lover beside him. Right now, his mother's face seemed open, expectant even, as if she were waiting for him to say it. He wondered again if she already knew.

"I . . . ," he began. He felt his hand beginning to sweat beneath hers.

"What?" she said. She leaned toward him. "What?"

His throat felt dry, scratchy. "I am," he said.

The pressure on his hand increased.

"You are what, Jim?" she said.

Her eyes were wet. Maybe from the salt air, Jim thought.

He said, "Yes. I am happy."

Eve's hand slipped off his, and settled back into her lap. There were circles of sweat under the arms of her mauve jacket. On the pocket she wore a rhinestone pin of an owl with glittering green eyes.

Suddenly the waiter was back with her water. He placed it in front of her with a flourish, then winked at Jim. Jim realized his heart was pounding, but he wasn't sure if it was from how close he had come to finally telling her the truth, or from the closeness of this blond man whose nametag read *Randy*.

"Thanks, Randy," Jim said, pronouncing the name with great care.

"Ugh," Eve said, spitting water back into the glass. "What's in here?"

Randy's face clouded. "Lemon," he said.

Eve slumped back into her seat, defeated.

"Maybe we could just take the check?" Jim said.

Randy nodded. When he returned with it, he slipped Jim a note written on a napkin. Their eyes met for just an instant. Jim's hands shook slightly as he read the note: "Call me?" and Randy's name and phone number. Jim looked up. His mother was staring at him. He glanced away from her, his eyes seeking out Randy. He saw him, across the patio, waiting. Jim gave him the slightest nod.

"Ready?" he said to his mother.

"What's on that napkin?" she said.

The sun had shifted and seemed to be boring right through Jim's skull. It made him slightly lightheaded. He shrugged.

Eve frowned at him. "I waited forever," she said.

"No, you didn't," he told her. "You were in the wrong place. I was right where I was supposed to be."

"No," she said. "You weren't."

Eve was supposed to stay for five days. But after three she told Jim she wanted to go home. "I don't like it here," she said. "A person can't even get a drink of water that tastes right. You can't walk anywhere. Always in the car. Drive, drive, drive. And everything seems wrong, smaller or something." She was disappointed in the stars' homes he drove her past, disappointed in the Hollywood sign, disappointed in the Ramos gin fizzes at the Beverly Hills Hotel. They saw Mel Gibson in a restaurant and she was disappointed in him too. "Even he's smaller than he seems," she said. Jim was afraid she was going to cry.

On the night she announced she was leaving on a flight the next day, Jim said, "Then we'll go out somewhere special for dinner."

But Eve shook her head. "We haven't spent any time together."

"Ma," he said, "we've been together constantly for three straight days."

"Not really. You've been keeping me busy all the time. So we don't have to talk."

"Don't be ridiculous," Jim said.

"Remember when your father left?" his mother asked him. Eve patted the couch beside her. Reluctantly, Jim went and sat there. She had on the mauve pantsuit again. Jim caught a slightly sour smell coming from her. "He sent us up to the lakehouse for a weekend and when we got back he had moved out."

"I remember," Jim said. He remembered how hot it was that night, how the crickets seemed to sing extra loud, cracking through the summer air. They had walked inside and found most of the furniture gone, the refrigerator empty, and a note. His mother had sat down on the yellow and green linoleum and sobbed. Jim was seven.

"In some ways," Eve said now, "you're like him."

"Thanks a lot," Jim said. "That's a real compliment. Especially knowing how you feel about him."

Instead of getting angry, his mother smiled at him, a small, sad smile.

"I'm not like him," Jim said. He had not seen his father in over ten years. Once, his father had taken him camping. To Jim, that was the last time they were together, although his mother told him he was wrong. Jim had refused to go to the bathroom in the woods and his father had yelled at him, taken him home early. "You disgust me," his father told him in the car. When they got to his mother's, Jim ran out of the car and up the walk. "You run like a girl," his father shouted after him.

"I said in some ways," Eve said. "The way you avoid talking about things, for example."

"Fine. I'll talk," Jim said too loudly. He jumped off the couch and stood before her, fists and jaw clenched. "What do you want to know?"

"Well," she said, "for instance, are you dating anyone special?"

"No," he said. That was the truth. He had been dating a man whose name, strangely, was also Jim. But they had broken up a few months back and the man had moved to Tucson.

"Are you dating anyone at all?" she said.

"Yes," Jim said, truthfully again. Last night, after his mother went to sleep, he had called Randy, the waiter, from the phone in his bedroom. They had talked for an hour and set up a date for Monday night. Jim was going to cook him dinner here.

"Who?"

"What is this?" Jim said. He recognized the shrillness in his voice. It was just like hers. "Even if I tell you, you won't know them. You don't know anyone here except for me, do you?"

Eve didn't say anything. She just sat there, waiting. Wasn't this what he'd brought her here for? To tell her? But Jim could not think of what to say exactly, or how to say it.

Finally he said, "Can we go to dinner now?" He felt exhausted. He felt like he could sleep for days without waking up. He imagined doing just that, crawling into bed and going to sleep. When he finally woke up, she would be gone, back in her own house with Debbie's picture smiling out at her, comforting her.

"Are you still a good cook?" Eve said, her voice soft.

"Yes."

"Cook me dinner then. It's our last night."

He grilled chicken coated with Dijon mustard, and potatoes. He tossed a big salad. They sat outside on his small patio to eat. Eve admired his garden, the lush tomatoes and baby lettuce. Jim drank too much wine on purpose.

"You know what's a shame?" his mother said. "That I have to fly back. I'm terrified."

"It's safer than driving in a car," he told her. He had told her that before she came too.

"I don't believe that."

"Well, it's true," he said, trying not to sound irritated.

"Don't believe everything you hear," she said. "How do you think those people felt when that bomb went off and they fell out of the sky?"

"What people?"

"All those people on that Pan Am jet. Flight 103. And right before Christmas. I saw all those mothers on TV who had lost children." She took a big breath. "There is nothing worse than losing your child. Nothing."

Drunkenly, Jim threw his arm around his mother's shoulders and placed a too-wet kiss on her cheek. "Well," he said, "you're stuck with me no matter what."

She laughed. "Stuck," she said. "Hardly. You're the one stuck with me."

The image of those unclaimed bags, circling, suddenly popped into Jim's mind again. He frowned, and the arm he'd tossed so casually around his mother tightened into a hug.

"Don't worry," he said. "No one wants to bomb a plane to Chicago."

She hugged him back, hard. "Oh, Jim," she said, "you're wrong. Bombs fall all the time. Unexpected. If people knew when they were going to drop, they'd avoid them, avoid getting hurt. Those people on that Pan Am plane, you think they would have gotten on had they known?"

"I don't know," he said. He held his mother at arm's length. She seemed ready for anything. But hadn't she just told him that a person wouldn't walk into a situation where a bomb was going to drop? He got up and moved toward the door that led inside.

"Where are you going?" Eve said.

He smiled at her, happy that she was sitting here on his patio at dusk, happy that tomorrow she would be gone.

"Dessert," he said. "The grand finale." And he went inside to get it, vanilla ice cream with cherries. He would come back out, pour cherry liqueur on top, then hold a match to it until, right before their eyes, it burst into flames.

"So," Jim said as they stood together at the airport waiting for his mother's flight to board, "Aunt Dodie will pick you up?

She'll be there waiting?"

Eve nodded. She had on a different pantsuit, a lemon yellow one with a pin of a clown on the lapel. Despite the bright color, the cheerful pin, she looked older, worried. Even when she smiled up at him, her frown did not disappear completely.

Jim watched a young couple kissing good-bye. The girl seemed hungry, starved even. His mother turned and watched too, as the boy kneaded the girl's rear end, pushing her into him greedily.

"Young love," Eve said, and turned away. Her frown deepened.

Jim could not take his eyes from them, from the curve of the girl's neck as she tilted her head, from the boy's slender fingers pressing her flesh. He wore a Yankees baseball hat, she wore floral leggings.

"Jim," his mother told him, "don't stare."

But he continued to watch. What would become of them? he wondered. They would grow up, fall out of love, never feel this way again. Or they would get married and grow to hate each other, forget this day when they could not bear to say good-bye. Maybe he would board this plane and it would get blown up. Maybe he carried the bomb himself.

"You're being rude," Eve said.

Jim sighed and turned away from the couple. His mother seemed to have shrunk in these few minutes since he last looked at her. She looked old, frail.

"Oh," she said, "I hate to fly. I'll never come to see you again, unless you move closer to home."

"I won't," he told her softly.

She looked out the window, at a plane taxiing in. "If you fall out of a plane at 35,000 feet, you vaporize," she said distractedly. "Zap! Gone. Just like that."

"Well, then, you'd better keep your seat belt fastened," he said. In that moment he decided he could not tell her. Not now, not ever. She was unable to handle it. She worried about sun exposure, vaporizing, bombs, and hijacking. At her own house, he knew, she had installed an elaborate alarm system. His mother was afraid to fly, afraid of everything. He saw again Debbie's face smiling out from on top of the television.

Eve tugged at his arm. "They're calling my flight now."

"I wish ...," he said, but didn't finish.

"I wish you could come with me, see me on the plane safely." She took her bag from him. "Will you wait here and watch until I've taken off safely? That way if the plane goes down, you'll be right here."

Jim had no intention of doing anything so ridiculous but he said, solemnly, "Yes. I'll wait right here." He kissed her quickly on the cheek. "Have a good trip. Have a Bloody Mary or something. Relax."

She began to move away from him, toward security. "Ha!" she said. "Easy for you to say. You'll have your feet planted firmly on the ground."

Jim waved good-bye. He turned, and the couple was gone, vanished, like they were never there at all.

Suddenly, his mother was back, standing right in front of him, her face close to his. "Jim," she said, "I think it's a shame that people can't be who they are. Whatever that is. If someone loves you, they don't care what you are. They love you no matter what. You have to be yourself. Be happy with who you are." She reached up and held his face in her hands. "There is nothing worse than losing a child. That's what they say. You're my only child, my boy. And I love you. I accept you for what you are. Do you know that?"

He nodded. He tried to speak but she was off again, walking away from him with great determination, like a small, lemon yellow soldier.

"Mom," he called after her. "Thank you."

She didn't look back. She just lifted her arm and waved, then disappeared down the long hall to her gate.

Slowly, Jim began to walk away. She had left two days early so he still had time off from work. He thought of calling Randy and asking him if he wanted to drive up to Big Sur for a few days. Yes, he thought, he would go home and do that. The loud roar of a jet engine revving made him stop. That would be his mother's plane, carrying her back home.

He turned and went back to the big window that looked out over the runway. Jim pressed his palms against the glass. His breath steamed a small O in front of him. The plane moved slowly down the runway, then picked up speed, and began to take off. Jim's heart beat hard against his chest as he watched. He realized he was holding his breath. Then the plane soared into the sky, lifting higher and higher, taking his mother upward, and away. Jim stood like that, palms pressed against the cool, smooth glass, eyes following the now speck of a plane, until he could no longer see it, and he was sure his mother would not fall from the sky.

Don Lee

Even then, a bit too serious for my own good.

Don Lee is a third-generation Korean-American. The son of a career State Department officer, he spent the majority of his childhood in Tokyo and Seoul. His fiction has appeared in *GQ*, *American Short Fiction*, and *New England Review*, and his nonfiction has been included in *The Village Voice*, *Harvard Review*, and elsewhere.

Lee lives in Boston and is the editor of *Ploughshares*.

Don Lee

Voir Dire

On Sunday afternoon, when Hank Low Kwon returned to his house in Rosarita Bay, he found a note tacked to his front door. "You don't think I *read*?" it said. The note was unsigned, but he knew it was from Molly. No doubt, she had seen the newspaper article, small as it was, summarizing the first day of the trial, and was miffed that he had mentioned it only tangentially to her. It was clearly his biggest case in three years as a public defender.

He had been working at his office all day and didn't know where Molly would be. He tried her at her loft, at the sports center and gym, and then, on a hunch, dialed the marine forecast—northwest at twenty knots, gusting to twenty-eight—and was certain he would find her at Rummy Creek, a windsurfing spot she'd discovered recently.

From the coast highway, he turned onto a dirt fire road that cut through a barbed-wire fence with no-trespassing signs, bumped down half a mile of scrub grass, wound past the Air Force radar station, and then arrived at the headlands bordering the ocean. Molly's truck was there, parked among a handful of cars, and Hank stepped to the edge of the cliff to look for her.

It didn't take long. She was flying across the water, feet in the board's straps, the sail raked so far back she was almost lying

Glimmer Train Stories, Issue 24, Fall 1997

flat—a human catamaran. She carved the board into a sweeping turn and raced back to shore. She jibed again, accelerated toward a wave, and launched off its lip, swooping fifteen feet into the air, and then touched down without missing a beat.

Hank sat on a tree stump and watched her. Molly had once described the feeling she got out there, sometimes flailing, struggling just to keep her balance, and then getting into a slot where everything fell into place, hydroplaning on the tail of the board, skimming over the chop. At that moment, going as fast as she could, it was effortless. She could take one hand off the rig, let her fingers drag in the water. She could look around, catch a little scenery—the cypress and pine atop the bluffs, the kelp waving underneath the surface. It was glorious, she had said, and as Molly, finished for the day, waded to the sand, as Hank climbed down the cliff to meet her, he could see the quiet elation in her face, the contentment of a woman who knew what she loved in this world.

But then she spotted Hank. She dropped her board and sail and marched toward him, sleek in her sleeveless wetsuit. Without a word, she punched her fist into his arm, stinging him so hard with surprise he fell to the ground. He gaped up at her, half laughing. "I can't believe you did that," he said.

"Did it hurt?"

"Yes, it hurt. Like a son of a bitch."

"Good. I feel better now," she said, and helped him to his feet.

The indictment was on two counts: Penal Code section 187, second-degree murder, punishable by fifteen years to life, and section 273a, subdivision 1, felony child abuse, punishable by one to ten. The previous summer, Chee Seng Lam, a cocaine addict, had beaten his girlfriend's three-year-old son, Simon Liu, to death with an electrical cord, whipping the boy, according to the medical examiner, more than four hundred times.

On Friday, before the weekend recess, Hank had given his

opening statement. He had told the jury that Lam was not a child abuser; he had never intended to harm Simon Liu that night. Indeed, he hadn't even known it was Simon he was hitting. High on cocaine, hallucinating wildly, he had believed he was lashing at—trying to protect himself from—a nest of snakes, thousands of them.

Drugs alone could not eliminate culpability. To win an acquittal, Hank would have to prove that the coke had made Lam delusional and paranoid, even when he wasn't under the influence—in other words, that he had developed a latent mental defect—and because of it, he was incapable of knowing or understanding the nature and quality of his act, or of distinguishing right from wrong—the legal definition of insanity in California.

"You believe him?" Molly asked as she hosed the salt off her gear in his driveway.

"I don't know," Hank said. "I'm not sure he's smart enough to have made it up."

"Does he have a history of violence?"

"Not against the kid, but yeah, he was your basic piece of shit." Chee Seng Lam had twenty-two prior arrests, mostly as a juvenile, when he had been a member of the Flying Dragons gang: aggravated assault, extortion, burglary, receiving stolen property, gun and drug possession, a couple of other assorted goodies, none of which would ever be revealed in court, since Hank had gotten his record suppressed.

"I guess you won't have too many character witnesses," Molly said.

"His dealer liked him."

Molly restrapped her shortboards on the rack of her truck. She had been a ten-meter platform diver in college, but she was in better shape now, at thirty-six, than she had been at her competitive peak, although most people never suspected it. Largely, this had to do with how little she cared about her looks.

She had a sweet, guileless face—eyes set wide apart, a plump mouth, long, wispy blond hair—yet she wore no makeup other than mascara, and her skin was always sunburned in patches, bruised, scratched, her lips chapped. In the rumpled sweaters and khakis she often wore, she was deceptively ordinary. Solid and thick-boned, one would think; maybe even a little overweight.

But of course, underneath the baggy attire, it was all muscle and power. Besides windsurfing, Molly skied, kayaked, rock climbed, and occasionally entered a triathlon for fun. She had degrees in biomechanics and sports science, and she was now the head diving coach at San Vicente University, where she had put together a championship program.

Her energy and fitness both attracted and overwhelmed Hank, who'd become, in his late thirties, a bit paunchy and prone to bronchitis. Yet, for all their differences, they got on remarkably well. They had been seeing each other for a year and a half, and recently they had agreed that they would move in together at the end of the summer, when their current leases expired. Both divorced, they were extravagantly careful not to attach undue significance to the decision. They knew enough not to ask the other for compromise, not to be too preoccupied about defining a future, which had become difficult of late, since Molly was now ten weeks pregnant.

She adjusted the nozzle on the garden hose and took a sip of water. "Would you mind if I came to the trial?" she asked.

"Why would you want to?"

"I want to see you at work. I've never been to a criminal trial."

"You might make me more nervous than I already am," he told her. This was partially true. Of the two-hundred-some cases he had handled, only fifteen had gone to a jury—a routine track record in the public defenders' office, where the motto was "plead 'em and speed 'em."

"Your ex-wife never went to court?"

"Didn't care for the clientele."

Molly pulled her T-shirt over her head.

"What are you doing?" Hank said.

"Rinsing the salt off." She bent over and sprayed water on her hair, then squeezed it into a ponytail.

Hank noticed a cut on her bicep. "You're bleeding," he told her.

She examined the gash, then licked the blood and kissed him. "Have you been smoking today?" she asked. "You taste like smoke."

"That's what I like about you. You don't nag. Why don't you put your shirt back on before someone gets a cheap thrill."

She looked down at her breasts. "Amazing. I actually have tits," she said. "They're so swollen. Feel them."

"Are they tender?"

"A little. You don't want to feel them?"

He handed back her T-shirt. "You really want to come to the trial?"

"Would it disturb you that much?"

"I guess not," he told her. "But it'll be embarrassing to watch."

"Why? Is your case that weak?"

"No, you don't get it," he said. "I think I'm going to win."

Last summer, on June 23, Ruby Liu drove down from Oakland to San Vicente with her son. She had been looking forward to spending the weekend with Chee Seng Lam, but right away they argued. Lam was irritated she'd brought Simon, and he berated Ruby throughout the evening about the boy's disruptive presence. "He say Simon noisy," she testified. "He say Simon need discipline."

Later, she and Simon fell asleep in the bedroom while Lam stayed up in the living room, listening to music on his headphones. At approximately 1 A.M., Ruby awoke and saw that Simon was no longer at her side. She walked down the hall and discovered Lam whipping her son with the cord to his headphones. She pushed Lam away. Simon was moaning, his eyes fluttering, and then he stopped breathing. She called 911. By the time the EMTs arrived, Simon was dead.

From the standpoint of the law, Ruby's testimony was devastating, but she wasn't entirely effective as a witness. She spoke in a rehearsed monotone, eyes down, body impassive and contained, and it was hard to fathom a mother not betraying a single hint of emotion as she related the death of her only child. She seemed to be hiding something. She seemed to be lying.

What everyone but the jury knew was that Ruby Liu was a prostitute and a junkie. She mainlined speedballs—a combination of heroin and cocaine—and she had gone to Lam's apartment that weekend to get high with him. She could have easily been indicted on a slew of negligence charges, so it was no surprise that she had agreed to testify for the prosecution.

"Did Mr. Lam ever hit Simon before?" Hank asked her.

Ruby glanced at the assistant district attorney, Marty Boudreau, then said no.

"Not once? Maybe an isolated spanking?"

"No."

"So he never hit Simon, or spanked him, or slapped him. Not once. He never even raised his voice to him, did he?"

"He say Simon noisy. He say he need discipline."

"You keep repeating that. Did he say this to you in English or Chinese?"

Ruby blinked several times, trying to choose. "English," she declared.

"How good would you say Mr. Lam's English is?"

"He speak English."

"Is he fluent, or is his English somewhat broken, like yours?"

"Same as me, maybe."

"Can he read and write?"

"Not good."

"Have you ever heard him use the word 'discipline' before?"

She squirmed a bit. "No."

"Are you sure he said 'discipline,' or did someone suggest the word to you?"

"Objection," Boudreau said.

For the next four hours, Hank had Ruby describe Lam's escalating drug use over the five years she'd known him, how eventually he would freebase cocaine for up to twenty hours at a time, sometimes going six days without sleep, obsessed with getting and smoking the coke, ignoring all else.

Increasingly, his behavior became more erratic. He saw bugs, tadpoles. On his body, coming out of his skin, on other people. Without warning, he would slap and scratch himself, claw his fingernails into his arms until he bled. Then he began seeing snakes. Diamondbacks, corals, water moccasins, copperheads, black mambas, cobras, tree vipers—he identified fourteen varieties from library books Ruby stole for him. Lam weather stripped his doors and sealed every window, covered the heating vents with screens. He would often drop to all fours with a flashlight and a propane torch, hunting for the snakes, burning the floor and furniture.

Once, he beat a sofa cushion with a stick, trying to kill the baby cottonmouths he said were slithering out of it, rending the cushion apart for an hour and a half without pause. He heard voices; he saw ghosts. He thought the government was dumping the snakes into his apartment to kill him, and he drilled peepholes in the walls, bolted a security camera above his front door, and installed listening devices in nearly every room. He would not leave his apartment. Repeatedly, Ruby tried to convince him that the cocaine was making him hallucinate, but he refused to believe her. She was crazy, he said.

"Was he freebasing cocaine the night Simon was killed?"

"Yes."

"When you discovered him standing over Simon in the living

room, did you yell at him to stop?"

"Yes."

"And did he respond to you in any way?"

"No."

"So he appeared to be in a trance?" Hank asked.

Ruby frowned. "I don't know," she said. "No."

"Like the time with the sofa cushion?"

"Asked and answered," Boudreau said.

Hank withdrew the question and said instead, "Where were the headphones?"

"What?"

"He was holding the cord to his headphones, but where were the headphones themselves?"

"I don't know. His neck, maybe."

"Mr. Lam often spent all night doing cocaine while he listened to music on the headphones?"

"Yes."

"Would you say, then, that when Simon walked in, Mr. Lam must have jumped up in a panic, thinking these snakes—"

Boudreau cut him off. "Calls for speculation, Your Honor," he complained, his face flushing. Boudreau had some form of psoriasis, and whenever he was nervous or rattled—which was all the time—his skin bloomed red. Boudreau asked only one question in his redirect: "Did you ever see Mr. Lam selling drugs?"

"Yeah, he sell drugs."

Hank stood up. "Did he sell drugs to make a profit," he asked, "or just to support his own habit?"

Ruby looked dumbly at Hank. She was exhausted. "Habit, okay?" she said.

After a lengthy sidebar at Hank's request, the judge, Eduardo Gutierrez, instructed the jury that the issue of selling drugs was pertinent only to the defendant's state of mind, not his character. "The fact that Mr. Lam might have sold drugs does not prove he has an inherent disposition to engage in criminal conduct," Gutierrez said, remarkably deadpan.

Lam wore a striped, button-down shirt, which was one size too large for him, a tie, and pleated pants—nothing too fancy, but neat. His hair was cut above the ears, and he was clean shaven. Since he was small and thin to begin with, he looked, by design, harmless—a far cry from the ponytailed, hollow-eyed menace to society Hank had met nine months earlier, when Lam had been released from Cabrillo State Hospital.

In a conference room next to the holding pen, Hank gave Lam a cigarette. Smoking wasn't permitted anymore, but everyone ignored the rule. "You do good," Lam said. "Better than I think."

"I covered all the necessary points."

"No, really. Before, I think you stupid."

Hank was used to this reaction. No one had any respect for public defenders—not judges, prosecutors, cops, not the public, least of all clients. "Don't get too smug," he said. "We've got a long way to go."

Lam blew on the tip of his cigarette, reddening the cherry. "Blondie your girlfriend?" Lam said. He'd seen Molly with Hank during a recess. "*Low faan* girlfriend, huh? No more like Chinese girl?"

Hank flipped through the pages of his notepad. He didn't want to go through this again with Lam, who had made a sport of referring to Hank's ex-wife.

Everyone in Chinatown knew Allison Wang—the former Miss California, the daughter of Councilman Jimmy Wang. They were affluent and very visible ABCs, American-born Chinese, and the Wangs' prominence was the main reason Hank had chosen San Vicente County's PD office over San Francisco's, why he rented a house in Rosarita Bay instead of living in the city.

In Chinatown, Hank was considered *juk-sheng*, "hollow as a bamboo pole," because he didn't know Chinese or anything about their culture. It didn't matter that he had been born and raised in Haliewa, on the North Shore of Oahu. It didn't matter that, although Kwon was a Chinese-sounding name, his father, a Presbyterian minister, was actually Korean, and his mother was a Hawaiian mongrel of Asian/Pacific origins—Chinese, Japanese, Samoan.

Lam helped himself to another cigarette. As he was lighting it, Hank noticed his eyes—glazed and dilated. "You're stoned," he said.

"Naw."

"Bullshit."

"Just a little pot."

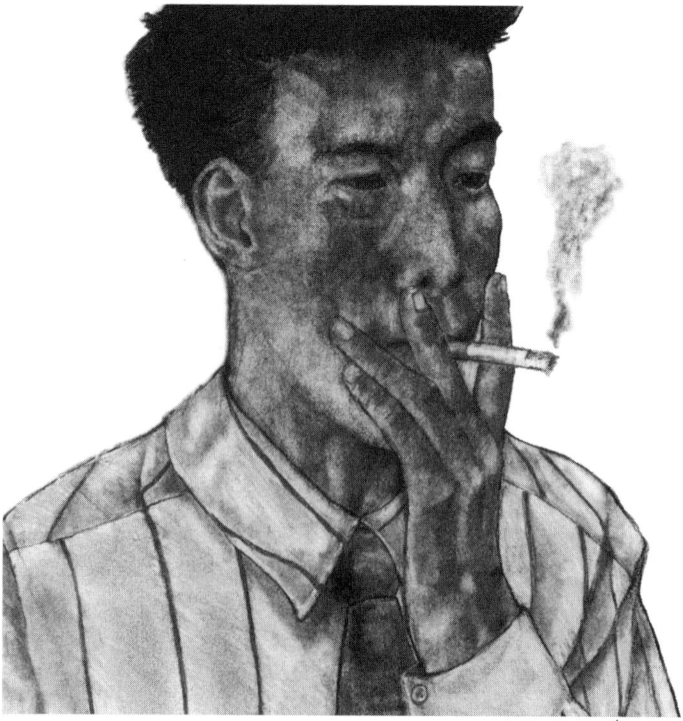

J. LEON 97-

"You idiot. I told you to stay clean."

"You see Ruby? I betcha Valium," Lam said. "Good thing I never marry her. She lie first, you know. Say Simon my baby. But I know. I slap her. 'My baby? My baby?' She cry. 'Boo hoo.' Mistake. Big mistake. You same? Why you and Allison Wang divorce? She make mistake, Hankie?"

Hank stared at Lam—grinning,clowning. "When we get back in the courtroom," he told him, "you don't smile, you don't laugh. You don't act bored or slouch in your chair. Look serious and remorseful. Look like you feel bad about what you've done."

After two days, Molly told Hank she wouldn't be able to attend the rest of the trial—she had more work to do than she had thought. This was an equivocation, Hank knew. Maybe she was bored by the fits and starts of the trial, the continual sidebars, the lags between witnesses. Maybe she was disgusted by Lam, and horrified that Hank was defending him. Whatever the case, he was relieved she would no longer be there.

"You won't miss much," he said to her over dinner at her loft.

"Do you think they assigned this case to you because you're Asian?"

"That's rhetorical, right?"

"Because they thought it'd help with the jury?"

"Partly them, mostly the client."

Molly picked at her food. "You ever wonder what makes people go in one direction and not another?"

"What do you mean?"

"All the little things that add up. I was thinking about Lam and his girlfriend, the model minorities they turned out to be. Aren't you ever curious about that?"

"I used to be. Not anymore."

"Why not?"

Hank wiped his mouth. "There's this strangely poetic phrase in the California Penal Code. Malice can be implied if circumstances show 'an abandoned and malignant heart.' Day in and day out, that's what I see. Some people are just evil."

"That's a charitable view of the world. I thought you were such a liberal."

"Given enough time, we all become Republicans." He told Molly about one of his first cases in juvenile court, an eleven-year-old kid who, as he was riding down the street on his BMX bicycle, swung a pipe into a man's face. No reason. Didn't know him, didn't rob him. Just felt like it. Hank found out some things about the kid's background—broken home, physical abuse—and thought he deserved another chance. A month later, the kid participated in a home invasion. He raped and sodomized a six-year-old girl with a broomstick, a beer bottle, and a light bulb, which he busted inside her, and then, for good measure, hammered a few nails into her heels. Immediately afterwards, Hank did something he thought he would never do: he bought a gun—a 9mm Glock—and he thought Molly should get one, too. She lived in a converted warehouse in downtown San Vicente, and her loft was cluttered with expensive computers and sports equipment and prototypes of exercise machines, which she tested as a sideline. It wasn't safe.

"I don't need a gun," Molly said. "I have you. My Moo—"

"Don't start."

"I have to pee," she told Hank. "It's incredible how many times I have to pee these days."

There was a mini-trampoline on the floor, near the foot of the bed, and on the way to the bathroom, Molly nonchalantly hopped onto it and did a forward flip. She grinned back mischievously at Hank. For a while, the trampoline had been an instrument of ritual. Whenever Molly wanted to make love, she would bounce off the tramp, tumble through the air, and flop onto the sheets. "Time to make Molly jolly," she'd say to Hank. Sometimes, growling: "Tiger Lily want her Moo Shi Kwon." At first, Molly's sexual assertion had unnerved him. When they began dating, she had been subdued and uncomfortable, and he had been certain, each time he called her, that she would not see him again. At the end of their fourth date—another disaster, he had thought—he drove her home and lightly kissed her cheek goodnight. She stayed in the car, cracking her knuckles. "That's *it*?" she suddenly blurted. "You mean you're *done* with me?" Then she had ravished him, taking him inside to the loft and stripping him of his clothes. With Molly, all roads originated in the body. Her entire life, she had spoken through it—joy found in challenging limits and conquering the elements, being fearless, perfect, indomitable. She needed the physical to achieve intimacy, and gradually Hank gave in to her. They became accustomed to not using anything at all, depending, more and more cavalierly, on Hank to withdraw.

She wanted a baby someday soon—he knew that—but he did not. Or so he had believed. He could not explain himself.

The roles had been reversed during his marriage. His wife, Allison, had not wanted to interrupt her career for children. She was rising fast, promoted to vice president at Kaiser Permanente before she turned thirty. Hank had been a reporter for the *San Francisco Chronicle* then, and when he decided to reduce his hours and attend law school at night, she fretted about money. "What's the point if all you're going to do is be a public defender?" she had said. She teased him, called him a bleeding-heart pagoda, and he joked that she was a born Chuppie, a Chinese yuppie. But privately they knew their marriage was fracturing, and Hank blamed much of it on Allison's self-absorption—epitomized, he felt, by her refusal to have children.

"That's what I've always hated about you," Allison had said. "Your moral superiority. What makes you think you're so much better than everybody else? I just don't like kids, okay? It might be un-Chinese, but for the life of me, I don't have a single maternal instinct. I look at a baby, and all I can think about is how much shit it expels from every orifice. I'm disgusted by them.

Does that make me a horrible person?"

"Yes," Hank had told her.

Yet, when Molly had revealed she was pregnant, Hank had said he would support her either way, but it would be her decision to make; it was too soon in their relationship for him to advise her, much less promise her anything. He wouldn't say it explicitly, but it was clear he favored an abortion.

He loved Molly. He thought they might get married eventually and spend the rest of their lives together. But having a baby with her was another matter. His job had changed him. Before, he had thought not wanting a child was selfish. Now, he thought wanting one was.

The photographs hurt. There were five of them—all color eight-by-tens—and they sat on Boudreau's table for the next two days as he called up the firemen who were first on the scene, the EMTs who tried to revive Simon, and the police officers who arrested Lam. With each witness, Boudreau brought out the photographs and asked, "Do they accurately and fairly depict the condition of the boy as you found him?" And each of these grown men, these veterans of daily, horrific violence, would wince looking at the pictures, then choke out yes.

Each of them confirmed that Lam had pointed to the headphone cord when questioned what he beat Simon with, that he had kept repeating he wasn't a child beater, and that though he seemed agitated, he was coherent, even asking to change his clothes and put on his shoes before being cuffed. He did not mention any hallucinations. Not a word about snakes.

The medical examiner testified that he had counted four hundred seventeen separate and distinct contusions and abrasions, and the cord was consistent with the injuries. At some point, he said, the cord must have been doubled up, which would explain some of the U-shaped marks. The official cause of death was swelling and bleeding of the brain, caused by trauma, which forced the brain into its base and cut off breathing functions.

"You also found a large lump on the back of his head?" Hank asked.

"A blunt-force injury on the occipital lobe."

"Was it caused by the cord?"

"No. Most likely he fell backwards to the floor and hit his head."

"He tripped and fell down."

"Or he was pushed."

"Could the fall have rendered Simon unconscious the whole time?"

"That's impossible to determine."

"Is it possible, however?"

"I suppose."

"Could the fall, bumping his head, have been the actual cause of death?"

The M.E., seeing where Hank was going, smirked and said, "Unlikely."

"But it's possible?"

Boudreau objected, and Gutierrez had them approach. "You know better than to challenge proximate cause," he told Hank. "Move it along."

Hank held up the plastic evidence bag containing the headphones. "It's been stipulated that this cord is ten feet long, but only one-sixteenth of an inch wide. With the headphones, it weighs less than three ounces. Wouldn't you say it's pretty ineffective as a weapon?"

"It seemed to do the trick."

"But considering how light it is, it's rather awkward to use as a whip, isn't it? Even doubled up?"

"I wouldn't know."

"Did the injuries indicate a repetitive motor motion?"

"Obviously."

"The same action, over and over, like a mindless robot?"

"I can't make that characterization."

"But you are an expert on injuries resulting from the application of specific weapons?"

"I am that."

Hank showed the M.E. two photographs of Lam's living room and passed copies to the jurors, which was decidedly risky, since they would spot the VCRs stacked in Lam's apartment and might surmise, correctly, that he had been fencing them. "If Mr. Lam really wanted to inflict pain, 'discipline' someone, as it were, wouldn't the baseball bat—right here in the photograph, right next to where they found the deceased—wouldn't it have been more effective?"

"That depends," the M.E. said.

"What about this broomstick here? Or this belt?"

The M.E. sighed. "Mr. Kwon, a piece of dental floss, tightened around a tender part of the body, could be more excruciating than many more obvious methods of torture. Its general innocuousness as an implement of hygiene does not remove its lethal potential. What happened to this boy was brutal, and it caused him unimaginable pain, and it killed him."

"Maybe wrong before," Lam said in the conference room. "Maybe you really stupid."

Hank lit a cigarette. Lam, wanting one, motioned to Hank, who ignored him.

"Hey," Lam said. "C'mon."

Hank forcefully slid the pack across the table, bouncing it off Lam's chest.

Lam tsked. "Be nice."

"Tell me something," Hank said. "How do you know Simon wasn't your kid?"

"Huh?"

"What makes you so sure he wasn't your son?"

"You crazy? Ruby whore. She slam heroin with needle. Always use condom."

"You had no feelings for him whatsoever."

Lam shrugged. "Make noise. Run run. Break stereo. Always cry. 'No food. No toy.' Little whore baby. Ruby no care. You think Simon become doctor? Maybe lawyer, like you? Better dead."

A few days ago, Hank had found a pregnancy book in Molly's loft, hidden in a cupboard. She had scribbled names in the margins: Rae Anne, Bethany, Thomas Graham, paired with Molly's last name, Beddle, then with Beddle-Kwon, Kwon-Beddle, and Kwon. Hank had read a passage in the book that she had underlined. At twelve weeks, the fetus would be fully formed. It would have eyelids, thirty-two tooth buds, finger- and toenails. It would be able to swallow, press its lips together, frown, clench its fists. It would be, at that point, two-and-a-half inches long.

"It sickens me to think I might let you walk," he told Lam.

"Too bad. You have job."

"I find myself asking what would happen if I slipped a little, made a mistake here and there."

"No choice. You have job. You do best."

"Maybe I already fucked up on purpose. You were right about the medical examiner. I'm usually smarter than that."

"No, you too much goodie-goodie. You never do that."

"No?"

"Naw."

"The funny thing is, you wouldn't be able to tell. No one would. If I'm not blatantly incompetent, no one would ever know."

Lam giggled, then slowly quieted down, growing uncertain. "Better not," he said. "Better not, you fuck."

"Who would it hurt?"

His defense took four days. He had a narcotics detective testify that, contrary to Boudreau's suggestions, Lam was not a dealer of any consequence. The paraphernalia found in his apartment was used for freebasing, a somewhat antiquated method of smoking coke, reserved for connoisseurs and hard-core addicts. Instead of heating cocaine-hydrochloride powder with baking soda, which would yield crack, Lam separated the base with ether and a propane torch. Freebase was purer than crack, but no dealer today went through the trouble of producing it. It took too long, and it was dangerous. And although crack houses had precision scales and surveillance equipment like Lam's, most dealers did not have any reason to monitor the inside of the house. There was also no currency found in the apartment, no vials or plastic pouches that were the usual receptacles for distribution.

Three of Lam's friends corroborated Ruby's testimony about Lam's bingeing habits, paranoia, and snake fixation, but all three, when cross-examined by Boudreau, were impeached rather comically. Each claimed he had never bought any drugs from Lam, never saw him sell drugs to anyone else, didn't know where he got them, didn't smoke with him, simply went to the apartment to watch TV.

A neighbor recalled seeing Lam scamper out to the street one evening in his underwear, bleeding profusely, screaming. She called the police, who took him to the hospital. Lam told the admitting nurse he'd run through a sliding glass door, trying to get away from the snakes. He was transferred to the county mental-health clinic, where he'd been held five previous times for acute cocaine intoxication.

The Chinese officer who had booked Lam on June 23 recounted their conversation in the police station. Lam spoke to him in Cantonese and insisted he had not known it was Simon he was hitting, he'd seen snakes, that he would have never done anything to hurt the kid.

Finally, Hank brought Dr. Jeffrey Winnick to the stand. Winnick, a psychopharmacologist, studied the effects of cocaine on human behavior. He was a frequent consultant to the FBI and the DEA, and he had testified in over five hundred trials, mostly—Hank emphasized—for the prosecution. By chance, Winnick had been doing research at Cabrillo State Hospital when Lam was taken there to test his competency. Over the course of four months, he interviewed Lam three times a week for a total of seventy hours.

"Did you arrive at an opinion about Mr. Lam?" Hank asked.

"In my opinion, Mr. Lam was psychotic on June 23rd and could not appreciate the wrongfulness of his actions. In my opinion, he did not know it was Simon he was beating."

He explained to the jury the psychopathology of freebasing. Because the surface area of the lungs is equivalent to a tennis court, smoking cocaine allows the drug to enter the bloodstream almost instantaneously, affecting the brain within eight to twelve seconds. The initial effect is as a stimulant, creating a feeling of confidence and euphoria. As one's tolerance increases, however, dysphoria occurs, prompting more frequent usage, which leads to paranoia.

"People often begin to have hallucinations at this point," Winnick said, "the most common of which is cocaine bugs. Their brains are firing so fast, these bursts of light—snow lights, they're called—flash in the corners of their eyes, and they think they're seeing things that aren't there, that keep escaping when they turn to look. At the same time, their skin feels like it's prickling, because cocaine constricts the blood vessels, and the combination leads them to believe there are things crawling on them—bugs or worms, or, as in Mr. Lam's case, snakes—and they'll scrape their skin or try to catch them. Since they're wide awake, they'll be absolutely convinced they're real, and they'll have delusions about them beyond the period of intoxication. This stage is referred to as cocaine paranoid psychosis, and it can be latent for months or even years after the last use of cocaine."

"Did Mr. Lam's cocaine habit progress to this stage?"

"Yes. His entire world revolved around trying to prove the existence of these snakes and trying to capture and kill them. He was terrified of them."

"Is cocaine paranoid psychosis caused by an organic disturbance to the brain?"

"Yes."

"So you would say that this is a mental defect?"

"Absolutely."

"Was Mr. Lam suffering from this mental defect on June 23rd?"

"I am certain that he was."

The jury took two days to reach a verdict, and in the end, they did what was right. Legally, they felt obliged to acquit Lam of child abuse, but they could not absolve him completely of killing Simon. Nor could they find him insane and send him to the relative comfort of a state institution. They convicted him of voluntary manslaughter. Gutierrez sentenced Lam immediately to the maximum term—eleven years.

Hank went to Molly's loft and told her the news. "I should resign," he said.

"Why?"

"I did a great job. On the evidence alone, the jury should've found him not guilty. But they didn't, and I'm relieved. What does that say about me as a public defender?"

"It says you're human. It says Lam got a fair trial."

"With early release, he could be out in six years. He killed a three-year-old kid. Is that fair?"

They went to a sushi restaurant around the corner for dinner, and then stopped by a store to rent a couple of videos before returning to the loft. Between movies—two stupid, mindless comedies Molly hoped would distract him—Hank popped in the videotape of Molly competing in the NCAA championships fifteen years ago.

"Why are you watching that again?" Molly asked, coming out of the bathroom.

The first time Hank had seen the tape, it had been a revelation, the image of her then. She had saved her best dive for last—a backward one-and-a-half with three-and-a-half twists, ripping the entry, barely bruising the surface. As the crowd erupted, Molly had pulled herself out of the pool. She had knocked the side of her head with the heel of her hand, trying to get the water out of her ear, allowing herself only a small, victorious smile.

"Can you believe I was ever that young?" Molly said. She moved over to the couch, straddled Hank's thighs, and sat on his lap. "I have something to tell you," she said, wrapping her arms around his neck. "I decided this a while ago, but I wanted to wait until after the trial. I've decided to have this baby no matter what. With you, without you, regardless of how you feel."

"I suspected as much."

"But I'm hoping you'll be there with me. Do you think you will be?"

Hank looked at Molly—her large blue eyes, the freckles across her cheeks, the blond down of eyebrows and lashes. "I don't know," he said. He thought of her standing on the ten-meter platform, not a single tremor or twitch, taut and immortal in her bathing suit. "Our worlds are so different," he said. "You deal with human beings at their highest potential. I see them at their worst."

"What does that mean?"

"How can I say I'll be able to protect this child, when I'm putting people like Lam back on the streets?"

"You can't. But that's the risk we'd have to take. Don't you think it'd be worth the risk?"

They watched the second movie, then fell asleep together. For how long, he did not know. A black, dreamless sleep. Then he awoke to the bed shaking. An earthquake, he thought, as he lay on his back, opening his eyes to the ceiling, scared.

But it was Molly, naked, standing over him at the foot of the bed. "Don't move," she said. He saw her body toppling, breaking the plane of inertia, then falling toward him, gathering speed as she brought her hands together, arms rigid, palms flat. An inch before his face, she split her hands apart, and he felt a rush of air as they brushed past his ears. "You ever play this as a kid?" she asked, holding herself over him. "Admit it. You want this baby."

"What are you doing?"

She stood up and fell again. "Confess."

"I can't be coerced," he said.

"You sure?" She got off the bed. "Don't move."

She walked to the middle of the floor, then turned around. She took two steps, ran toward the trampoline, and bounded into the air. Her back was arched, arms swept out in a swan dive. She was coming right at him. He watched her, staying still. She was going to crush him, he knew. Eventually, she would crush him.

JOAN HAWKINSON BOHORFOUSH
Radio-Documentary Producer

Interview

by Linda Burmeister Davies

Joan Hawkinson Bohorfoush

Joan Hawkinson Bohorfoush earned her M.A. in cultural anthropology from the University of Massachusetts. For her thesis, she produced a taped slide show on the history of American family life. She has taught global studies and U.S. history at the high-school level, American studies and women's history at Portland State University, and has developed slide programs for presentation to community and classroom groups. Bohorfoush produces radio programs on cultural and public affairs in Portland, Oregon, where she lives with her husband, Joe.

DAVIES: What I want to pursue, overall, is how your life has influenced your work.

BOHORFOUSH: Good.

You could have all kinds of labels, doing the work you do: maker of documentaries, writer, teacher, feminist, radical activist, anthropologist. What did I miss?

Well, I see myself not so much as an anthropologist but more as a humanist, and someone who has been able to bridge gaps, travel between different worlds. My own childhood was quite different from those of my friends. I grew up in a very religious home, a real unique home. In some ways it prepared me for my activism and my political consciousness. You can say some bad things about fundamentalism, but one of the good things you can say about fundamentalism is there's a lot of passion. And our family was a very close family. Our dinner-table conversations were about predestination and free will, so we cut our intellectual teeth there. I see myself as a free thinker even though I grew up in a home that didn't allow a lot of free thinking. Ironically, even though my parents were devout evangelical Christians and they didn't want us to question the Bible, somehow, at the same time, they gave us the message that they wanted us to be deep—whatever that meant to them. They scraped and saved and put us all through college, and that was their big unfortunate undoing, because eventually, especially as I studied anthropology, I began to study world religions and symbolism, and religion as symbolic behavior, and that started me thinking. It was the beginning crack that started to make itself seen, but it took a good ten years of intensive self-therapy and psychotherapy and plain suffering, to try to live both in the world of ideas and the world of humanism—secular humanism—but also not reject my parents, not lose my parents.

Because you did love them and it doesn't sound like they were repressive at all.

No, unlike some fundamentalist homes where religion is sort of shoved down people's throats in a cruel way, a real repressive way. For my parents—for them—it's what saved them, what got them out of the Depression mentally, and what got them through a lot of loss and grief and gave them vision. They were visionaries.

That's a nice thing to be able to say about your parents.

They were. I'd say both of them were visionaries and they both wanted a lot for their children, so they kind of sowed the seeds of our disbelief without knowing it. My oldest brother, Don, is the only one who's maintained the faith. He's an evangelical missionary, basically, and my youngest brother, Randy, also has belief, but it's a pretty private belief. But the three women, the three girls in the family, we all eventually went off in a different direction and in some ways, well, some people would say, "You went from Jesus to Marx."

It's not the same relationship, though.

No, I didn't want the deep, deep love of Marx as I had wanted this ... well, you know how a person in their teenage years can become very passionate about religion. You know how kids are. And I think for girls it's a replacement for sexuality and intimacy with other people, and it fulfills in a lot of ways. But when I was fifteen and my youngest brother was thirteen—all my older sisters and brother were out of the home by then—my father had a head-on collision which almost killed him. It was this terrible accident. That was a traumatic experience. You never could go back to the way it was, because my father never was the way he was.

But he didn't die.

He didn't die. We watched him claw his way back from near death. They said he would never walk again. They said he would never work again. He did both. He was a determined Norwegian man. Both my parents were Norwegian. My father's family were fishermen; they lived off the coast, fished out in the North Sea. But even my mother, who grew up on a farm in Norway Valley, in northern Alberta—you had to have grit to survive. Her family life was very different from my father's in that her father was a farmer and didn't have a lot of affection, or didn't express a lot of affection to his children. Her mother did; the mother was this matriarch—Ma, we all called her Ma—and she was an incredibly religious woman.

So your mother came to her religion from her mother.

But then again in the 1930s, both of my parents were caught

up in the tent-revival movement and they both found God again, in those troubled times, and that really bound them together. My dad's father was one of these other ... I see kind of two types of Norwegian families: the farmer family where the farmer is out there in the field and they adore their wives, but the children are the workers, the inside workers and the outside workers. Then you have fishing families where the father is gone for, sometimes, in the old days, six months at a time and the mother takes over the farm, because usually they have little farms that run down to the sea, and the mother becomes extremely competent. My grandmother was also competent, but she also deferred to Pa. Pa was a very strong, patriarchal man. But in the fishing families, with the father being gone so long that their authority dwindled, the mother, who has had to keep things under control, had to become the authority figure. Whereas the father, when he comes home, he's like Daddy Christmas. The children adore him. I've seen this pattern in a lot of Norwegian families that I've interviewed. My dad's family was that way. My dad was extremely affectionate. We would sit on his lap until his dying day, even in our twenties. He was just very affectionate, and his father was very affectionate, but his mother was very stern. She had to hold it together. There was a lot of anxiety, not knowing if her husband would return. So I see those strains, those sort of contradictory strains in our family. And the thing about having a vision and also caring for the world, even if it meant ... we were always afraid that God would call us to go to the mission field. We dreaded it.

What do you mean by that?

The idea of a calling. That you would be called to go to Africa or go to wherever to save souls. My oldest sister was a missionary in Africa. She was a nurse.

And God called her?

Well, it's a mental thing where you feel you have a calling to serve the Lord in foreign places.

I wonder how she experienced that calling.

It's totally subjective. It's like speaking in tongues. Our family wasn't a Pentecostal family, but a lot of my relatives were, my cousins. It's sort of like that. When the spirit descended on them, tongues would fly, would move, would just jabber. But I remember growing up and being afraid that God would call me to someplace I didn't want to go. I didn't want to be a missionary because they didn't seem to have much fun, and this, after all, was the sixties. I was born in '51. When I was fifteen, you know, the 1966 election year, my dad was in a head-on collision. I didn't see him for four months, neither my brother or I did because his head was swollen so big. He broke practically every bone in his body except for his hand. That was the only thing you could distinguish as belonging to the original man. He had had a real distinctive face. He's what you call a dark Norwegian. There's a whole folklore about that: that many years ago, Persians leaving the falling Persian dynasty traveled to Norway, and went to Karmey, up where my father's family lived, and intermingled with the village maidens, and you have a population of really dark Norwegians with Middle Eastern features and black, wavy hair—that was my father. All three of us sisters have been drawn to either Jewish men or Mediterranean men. In my case, I married a man of Lebanese descent. None of them looked Norwegian. We really did idolize my dad, and part of it was just his ability to always be up. He lost so much during the Depression. He lost his sister to TB, his brother to another illness; when he was ten his father died of stomach cancer and they were thrown into poverty, but my dad had an incredible sense of humor that I think he actually taught my mother. My mother was real reserved, but my dad was very expressive. It's too bad he didn't have more of an education. He did get an education when they were living in Alaska. He wrote away to the LaSalle Correspondence School and got his accounting degree. Straight As. It took him three years. This is while they were running a power plant, the two of them, in Alaska. Both of my parents, I could say, were adventurers and had a sense of real integrity. I mean, my mother's father did not come to her wedding because he thought it was so frivolous that during the Depression, when there was so much poverty, she would buy a nice dress and have a church wedding.

That must have been sad for her.

It was very sad for her. She worked as a house maid and saved all her wages to buy a satin dress. It meant so much to her because she was the first one in the family to have a church wedding, but her father didn't show up. I know it was painful for her, but my mother, who seemed demure and reserved, had a reservoir of strength that matched my father's. I think my father had more confidence. He was six foot four and he had an outgoing personality.

When this thing happened with your dad—I mean, fifteen is such an age.

It's a very tender age.

There's a certain amount of needing to separate from your parents and, as a girl, maybe particularly from your mother. To have this awful thing happen must have affected you deeply. When you look back, can you see—if that whole thing had not happened—who you'd be?

I really don't know because it so shaped me into what I became. For one thing, it made us a new family, in a sense, when my father did go back to work. I watched this man come back to life, and I saw my mother take the helm. I got a real lesson in endurance. Something that I'm learning now. I think I have my father's grit, in fighting disease, in surviving a long-term illness and fighting for your life. My dad had an incredible life force and I identified with that. Otherwise, I may have ... I mean I had just discovered the Beatles two years before and the sixties were swirling around us. I think I may have just become really caught up in the sixties and the protest movement, which I didn't. All of that disappeared for me. The Vietnam War disappeared.

Everything was, "You've got to save our father." And then it became, "Save our family," when we then moved to Sunnyvale, California. The company he had worked for was a small airline, and they were bought out by Hughes—the beginning of the merger days—and as soon as my father was barely well enough to pick up his job in a part-time way, they moved the company to San Mateo, California. I had been a sophomore when my dad was hurt and then it was the summer between my junior and senior years. I had grown up with these people and this school and we were secure there.

I bet that was hard.

Oh, it was very wrenching, but you know, I didn't give it a second thought because I had such incredible loyalty to the family. We could have stayed. We could have stayed with my aunt and uncle but ... And my younger brother, who was fourteen at that time—we were really concerned about him. It was just my brother and me and my parents. My three older brother and sisters were all off—married, in college, gone—and so, like I said, we formed a new family. I felt like my parents needed me to hold the family together, and I felt Mother ... You know, it was so hard on her, because my dad never looked like the man that she knew. I mean, his whole face just flattened out because of the head-on collision. He lost his laugh lines. He became very nervous, like someone who's been traumatized by a terrible injury, but she rose to the occasion, yet I knew she needed me. In some ways, I felt proud because my other sisters I don't think developed as close a relationship to my mother. My mother was always working, ironing, cleaning, taking care of kids, and I think they never felt they got quite enough of her.

So the two of you became close allies.

Exactly. And also we became allies in exploring this new world. And this new world, Silicon Valley, was a wasteland, a complete cultural, visual wasteland. And we had come from north Seattle, just an hour away from our relatives, because my family came from Skagit Valley and Bellingham. To be cut off like that. We clung to each other. My mother really depended on me, and I felt like there was a kind of quality to the closeness that I had that my sisters never had with her, and she then had a hysterectomy, at some point, and was ill from that. The other thing was that my youngest brother, Randy, hated California and he was having trouble in school. The school was totally alienating—four thousand students. He came from a school with one thousand kids, and these were the Reagan years in California—'68, '69. I graduated in '69. And they had this module system which seemed really modern, but it meant that if you didn't know what you were doing, you could just wander off campus, and my brother would, and, of course, then he'd be caught and be disciplined. It was just this terrible cycle, vicious cycle for him. Meanwhile we joined this church, which—little did we know—was also going to suck us into this vortex. It was called the Community Chapel.

It sounds so innocuous.

It sounds very benign, but it wasn't. It was almost like ... I don't know. It was more than a chapel. It was huge and they drew in a lot of lost kids. I mean, the sixties were in full bloom and people were coming back from Vietnam. I was aware of that and I was aware of the protest movement, but again, I wasn't political, and I certainly wasn't tempted by the drug movement, because life was scary. Plus, in the Community Chapel I was sort of a leader in the youth group. I played my guitar; I was this angel. I counseled. I don't know what I was talking about, trying to counsel kids that were trying to come off drugs, but it felt like we all had our fingers in the dike and the dike was about to break. It was cultural revolution. The sixties was happening around us, and we couldn't contain it, and yet, in this little church—this very big church, actually—we tried to stem the tide of all of that. I remember being terrified by drugs because of my friends and my younger brother and the kids coming into the church. I could see them drifting So in answer to the original question, had I not been torn from normalcy, from a normal adolescence, I might have just followed the way of the sixties. I might have experimented with drugs. It was years and years later that I experimented. But at the time, it was like I had to keep so vigilant and I had to be a good girl, a strong, good girl. And I was, in a way, the cop of the family with my brother, which was really hard on our relationship. We bonded real closely later when I left. I went to this Christian college, Westmont College, which my parents couldn't afford, but sent me to. It's a Christian liberal-arts college—again opening the door to more free thinking and more humanistic thought. I loved that college, but it was so ironic. In 1970 with the Nixon bombing of Cambodia, and Kent State and all of that, there was tremendous rioting in Isla Vista, the University at California in Santa Barbara, and they burned the Bank of America building, and I remember watching from our tower, our ivory tower, our beautiful little campus up there in the hills of Santa Barbara where the Reagans lived—which I didn't realize at the time—looking down and watching the Bank of America building burning and not understanding. I hadn't made that connection. So I was always trying to make that connection, but I felt marginalized by the sixties, and frightened. I spent two years at this college, went to Europe for a semester abroad, which was a seminal experience for me. We went to the Middle East and to Jerusalem, and we also went to East Germany, and I got to go to Buchenwald. I think that's when the crack really widened. How could God allow this? I didn't see this reaction among my classmates—this tremendous problem. I'm sure many of them did struggle with it. I began to read and read. And I really struggled with the contradictions between my faith and the world around me, especially looking at history and other cultures. I felt like I kind of had a sort of mini-nervous breakdown in Europe because it just came hurtling down upon me.

Some of the belief that you had based so much of your life on was suddenly jeopardized.

Yes, and knowing that if I gave that up, I would not only give up the rock of my own identity, but my parents and I would be on different planets. In fact, that's what happened when I did give up the faith. It took a long time. My sister Jan and I struggled together over these issues throughout our twenties. We were, and are, very close. My father came down with cancer when I was in college. I transferred to the University of Washington and he died in '76. I was married to my first husband. I was pretty much not an evangelical Christian at that time, but I wasn't an atheist either. When my father died, I was studying cultural anthropology at the University of Victoria with this professor who'd come straight from Chile. He was exiled from Chile after the fall of Allende, and he taught Marxism openly in the classroom. Dialectical materialism. I'm taking notes and looking around thinking, *Do all these other people realize what he's teaching?* But it was Canada, and there was a different point of view, and they weren't as shocked by radicalism. They didn't have that McCarthyist background. Plus, Jan had been studying Marxism from a different angle—critical theory, which is much more intellectual Marxism, and she had always challenged me intellectually. I came to a left perspective via anthropology, reading Frederick Engel's *The Origins of the Family, Private Property, and the State*, and, by golly, it made sense; but I could, of course, never admit to my parents that I was a Marxist, let alone a nonbeliever.

And yet from your work, it seems you actually carry on—in your own way—the concerns that a sincere fundamentalist might have. Really caring about the fates of other people.

In my family—I mean I look at my brother Don, deluded as I think he is, or misguided I guess is a better way of putting it. The man does not value material possessions. He does not value profitability, making money, or being powerful. He values making the world a better place, but his real agenda is to save souls. But I wanted *this* world to be a better place for its own sake. There's a fine line because a good missionary can sometimes be an advocate for the people's temporal struggles to make this world a better place.

It doesn't seem—if you believe yourself to be working on behalf of a benevolent god—that you could ignore people's suffering on any level.

Exactly. And if you've grown up with this idea of a benevolent god, and then had to deal with the problem of evil and of suffering, your whole life would be marked with both a concern for suffering and also an ability to tolerate contradiction. In fact that's what really appealed to me in Marxism—the notion of contradiction and paradox. That something can be this and that at the same time. Because I knew that all my life, and I lived that. I *was* this and that. And I saw that my parents, though they were devout evangelical Christians, were the kindest people you could ever imagine, and also welcomed my intellectual development even though, again, they didn't realize it would lead me away from them.

But it didn't. I mean I can see where in so many ways you're in the same place on a different path.

But there was such a set of concrete beliefs, with the Bible being the literal word of God, and once you give that up, once you give up a little part of it, the whole thing starts to crumble—and that's what's so scary about questioning a little part of it. You end up having to throw the whole thing aside.

Which is kind of a sad limitation.

It is a sad limitation. And I don't see it in, like, Catholicism, or in my friends who are Muslim, or other religious people—Jews who are able to pick and choose, Christians, too, who have very different interpretations.

There's more room.

But this one has very little room. And if you didn't pop out, well—I felt I would self-destruct. Because even if my parents weren't repressive, there was something inherently repressive about the whole belief system. It's anti-sexual, anti-intellectual, authoritarian, and I couldn't breathe.

Are you proud of the fact that you managed to choose?

I'm very proud. Because it required a great deal of suffering and it required a great deal of thought, and also pain, because it separated my mother and me. It caused her terrible grief because she could no longer speak the same language as me or as Jan. My sister Linda is more New Agey, so she can sort of speak the language. And now that I'm ill, it's very, very hard for my mother to not want to talk about my salvation, because in her heart, deep in her heart, she has this terrible fear that she won't see me again if I should die. It's this terrible thing. Fundamentalists, when someone gets sick or is perceived about to die—I'll never forget when my cousin Kay died of pancreatic cancer ten years ago. She wasn't like a free thinker, she was a party girl; she wasn't a Christian girl, and they made her repent. And I swore I would never do that, never do that. But at the same time, I can feel the pressure now. When my cousins call and they want to come and to be with me, my husband goes, "No, no, no. She's too weak." And I know my religious cousins want to come and pray around me. I know what they want. I can smell someone trying to save my soul. And having been a soul saver, I was a little missionary myself in a small way—summers: I went off one summer between my sophomore and junior years, I worked on an Indian reservation off the coast of Vancouver Island and played my guitar and ran a Sunday School, and we were in gear, we were in training to be missionaries, and that was a great honor. But there was also that fear of where you would end up. In any case, I was proud that I made that journey, but it was also a slippery slope, because I had to find a new paradigm. I think that's where my cultural anthropology helped me, and later my radicalism helped me. I went back and studied under some pretty famous Marxists back east, at the University of Massachusetts, and got a master's there in anthropology. There were some people there who were real great minds in economics and anthropology, and one of the women—Jonnetta Cole, who's now president of Spellman College—took us all to Cuba. It was during the Carter years. I was still married to a man named George who was a fisherman, and fortunately we fished during the summertime, so we had money. I was the deckhand. We had lots of money to go to school, so I did go there two years, and then we went to Cuba. And again, in some ways, I had that same kind of fundamentalist rah-rah spirit that I had to get knocked out of me a bit where I was a little too idealistic. I wasn't critical enough of Marxism and of socialism. I hadn't really developed that. But then I became a feminist. That was in the mid-seventies, and then I divorced my husband George. We were divorced in 1980: another turning point year for me. Mt. St. Helens went off, Ronald Reagan was elected, and John Lennon was killed. And I met Joe, who turned out to be a prince of a man, a wonderful man, who was younger than myself: he was still in college. I was an unemployed anthropologist. I wasn't an anthropologist, but I was out of graduate school and I worked as a waitress for quite a few years, and I had a taste of the working life. In any case, during that experience back at Amherst—I had done a slide show on the history of "the family." That was my dissertation. I wrote the script and put together all these slides and I gave a presentation to the faculty; that got me interested in media and how pictures and words could really have an impact. Even a simple little slide show could have a tremendous impact. So I came back to Seattle and I started showing it to different groups. Again, I was a little missionary, showing my slides like the missionaries that come back and show their slides. It had dialectical materialism woven through it. You didn't realize you were seeing dialectical materialism, but I tried to give an analysis of the rise of the nuclear family and how it wasn't just a bad thing. It was also a good thing. It was a way that people had, you know—again, looking at the good and the bad. From a feminist point of view, the patriarchal family was very oppressive; the nuclear family had taken on such horrible meanings. I tried to disentangle all of that. And then I met up with these two filmmakers in Seattle who offered to turn my slide show into a film. And that led me on the road to media even further. Turns out I chucked my slide show, and we came up with the idea of doing interviews with five families, where there were four generations of women from five different ethnic groups living in the Puget Sound area. A Norwegian family, a black family, Sephardic Jewish, Snoquamish Indian—I spent a lot of time on a Snoquamish reservation—and a Japanese family. We went back to one of the internment camps. I did all of the preliminary interviews. By this time I had met another very important person in my life, my friend Dina Dickerson, and she quickly got involved in this project with me, partly behind the scenes. The two producers, the filmmakers who had all the equipment, basically sent me out to do all the interviews, and then they would shape them into a film. These were all pre-interviews, so I didn't get good audio. Except with the Snoquamish. We still have incredible, incredible audios. But this woman, Dina, also like Joe, just changed my life. Because she became not only my very dear friend, but also my intellectual partner. We visionized together, we wrote together. It was like there was a chemistry. And we secretly plotted against these other people—it was our idea of what to do with this project. And Dina and I did, in fact, write the script. Dina is a programmer, a real accomplished computer programmer, and she ended up actually compiling all of these stories and we had umpteen hundreds of stories—and she catalogued them as Great Depression and coming-of-age stories, and she had them all in notebooks and computerized. She was—is—a very logical person. So she and I together transcribed the tapes and wrote the script. We had already done a lot of shoots, videotaping as well. We presented kind of a rough draft of the script, which was this epic thing, a family history, a weaving together—like *Lonestar.* I mean that was a great movie, but that was our vision. One insight we got from these four generations of women, twenty women, was that the time when a person comes of age, the time when you first begin to see beyond your own backyard and into what is happening in the world, this time imprints itself on you and you are that person for the rest of your life. Each generation was stamped, culturally, with an identity depending on when they first came of age.

That's sobering, isn't it?

It was, but it was also quite incredible that there's some pattern in human behavior and thought and consciousness. So anyway, we presented this script, and the producer said, "Well, I'll take it and I'll work with it," but she wasn't going to give us any credit. It was just going to be *her* story. My name might be on it, but Dina was going to be aced out because the producer felt threatened. I had thought they were comrades. I really did. But they weren't. They were using me to do all this work on this film and they were going to make of it what they wanted, and not give Dina credit. I walked away after working intensively for three years.

Three years?!

For no pay. It was my oldest sister that basically supported me. I lived with her, and I worked as a waitress. Nineteen eighty-two to '85, almost three years.

Three years? How did that happen?

I just got caught up. It started with my slide slow. I was so caught up, both Dina and I were caught up—my friend is a visionary, too, and when she gets a dream, she hangs onto it—and we thought this was just going to be the most incredible piece of work. Five families. And documenting the Snoquamish Indians—we had stories of when the original white boats, the first white traders, came around the bend of Puget Sound. We had stories of that, not that this grandmother herself was there, but she remembers stories her grandmother told of going down into the boat, and she would say, "They had red measles and purple measles and black measles, and our people would just get right down in the ship with them and we'd all just die." We had these stories. That's what kept us in there. The material was special, so rich. And then I married Joe in 1985 and we moved from Seattle to Portland, partly to get away from all that. Because I had to walk away from that project, which was very painful. I really thought I was a filmmaker. There's something very seductive about being a filmmaker. I had to eventually settle on radio: *Oh, radio, who cares about radio?* But I ended up with all of the audio tapes. My friend Dina paid for the lawyer; we thought we would teach them a lesson. We got an intellectual-property lawyer and Dina spent thousands of dollars to try to get our control of the project. Well, all we got was the tapes, and we got to kind of tell them off over the phone—that was it. It wasn't enough. It was a real traumatic experience for me. It took me years, *years*, to get over that. So when we got to Portland, I was just kind of floundering, working in various offices. But I wanted to be in Portland, because my sister Jan was here, and my friend Dina was here, and there was also a community of activists, and I immediately got involved in that. And that's when my political education really took shape. I mean it had before, in the seventies, with feminism and Marxism, but it was academic, and that's different. I had been a graduate student studying Cuba, and now I was on my own, and ... well, I was married, but ... My first husband did adore me and was a great person, but I never felt that he saw me as his intellectual equal, whereas my second husband did. We were very much equals, and so I just felt like I could really be myself. It was wonderful. It's been wonderful. I think it was in 1987—Central America was going on—in one of our discussion groups, we had this idea: Why don't we have a variety hour and all of us contribute pieces? We formed the Old Mole Variety Hour on KBOO radio. So I was sort of a founding member of that. It's been on ten years. It started before the Jesse Jackson election. We took it very seriously. At the same time, I was working for Central Catholic High School in the development office, and fine-tuning my not-so-great secretarial skills, learning computers, and also learning that I could probably be as good a teacher as these teachers, which sparked my interest in going back to school and becoming a teacher.

Sensible for someone who's grown up needing to teach.

And to affect people's lives. And I had really become affected by what had become sort of a theme in a lot of my radio work—how ordinary people's lives can make incredible differences. You don't have to be famous, you don't have to be Gloria Steinem or Fidel Castro. I sort of hit on this thing from *The Family Pictures Project*, our film. All of these families were ordinary, not famous in any way, and yet their stories would just blow you away. The courage, surviving Minadoka, surviving racism and poverty. That really struck me as being something that I wanted to promote, in my life, and to somehow give voice to more people like this. And if I couldn't do it with film, maybe I could do it with radio. So then we went back to our original tapes and put together a radio piece, and I could do another slide show because I did have pictures. And teaching. Teachers are ordinary people and I always thought I'd love to be a teacher. I thought I could be a really great teacher. I certainly had a lot to teach. And I like teenagers. I've always gotten along really well with teenagers. I don't have kids myself, but my nieces and nephews have made up for that. When they're teenagers, you can treat them like normal people. I just had that ability, I think. So for three years, Central Catholic gave me time off to get my teaching degree, and a lot of my master's work got transferred, and I took classes and I got my certification to be a social-studies teacher. So in 1989 I was a student teacher with this really wonderful teacher at Grant High School named Tom McKenna, who's considered one of the best social-studies teachers in the city, and it was a bit daunting because the kids all loved him. He was also the basketball coach and he was funny—a stand-up comic. Oh my god, he was a hard act to follow. But I could see what an incredible teacher can do, because they gave him all the kids who were kind of throwaway, that they'd kind of given up on, and he would turn them around. He taught them to have a voice. I came in during the middle of the school year, so I never saw the beginning where everything's kind of rough and ragged. But I saw the ending, where they were in a circle all reading a poem by Langston Hughes, and they would comment, and I was just blown away by the wisdom and the powerful voices that these students had, that this teacher had allowed, and he was my model. That summer I got a job in a social-studies department in the suburbs where they'd managed to kick out the coaches. The teachers in the department were mostly women, and they were doing cutting-edge pedagogy, really new approaches to teaching, and they had gotten word of me and had invited me to come out and apply for this job, this opening. But I jumped too soon. I didn't realize that this little social-studies department, this world of free thinking, was totally at odds with the community and with the student body, which were hyperconservative. And the administration.

You didn't recognize that because you walked into the school from this other perspective.

Yes. But I was totally open, as I've always been—*This is my vision, my vision of teaching*, and they hired me. There were a few naysayers, administrators who had doubts from the beginning whether I would fit the school. And they had doubts about the whole social-studies department, which I didn't realize was an experiment. It was a Camelot. It was not to last. It was very sad. I taught for three years there. It was 1989, just as the Persian Gulf War and Desert Storm were heating up and my job was to teach senior global studies. My first unit was on the Middle East and

Should we go to war? Let's talk about it. Little did I know I took my life in my hands. I felt terrified. Plus I had an Arab name, a name they knew as Arab, and they saw me as a liberal. They didn't know what a radical was, liberals were bad enough, and they associated me with all the other liberal social-studies teachers: "Oh, here's another one." The students had just gotten rid of this one teacher the year before, had driven her out in tears. They had tormented her. She lasted one year. There were a lot of wonderful students there, but there were a lot of real conservative students with parents who were very powerful in the community.

So they knew how to exercise power.

Yes. Through the administrators. I remember that first semester was horrible because we really got into the Middle East and Islam, which, by the way, is what then piqued my interest in Islam later on. But I would bring in speakers from both sides. I brought in speakers from the PLO. I brought in rabbis. Recruiters, as well as defectors. Vietnam vets against the war. So I know I rattled their cages. And I know it made it very anxious for these students, so they kind of tried to torment me, but my Norwegian grit—the more fire that's under me, the hotter I get, and the more I will keep fighting back. And it seemed like every year was a different fight, and by the third year I was up for tenure: I thought I'd finally established myself. I'd gotten good reviews and I had a really good following of students and I was doing good things in the classroom, but they decided midyear that they didn't think I was going to make it; they didn't think I was tenure material. I went straight to the union and I got a lawyer, and I fought it. I was under surveillance for about five months. Surveillance in the sense that they put me on a "plan of action"—I had been on a "plan of assistance" at the very first because I'd caused all hell to break loose in my classroom with the war and everything. I mean, I suppose I didn't always handle it right, because I was so mortified by this war. I'd be out there at the candlelight vigil every Friday night, and there'd be other teachers and some students, and then I'd go in on Monday and it was a real emotional time.

You were fully involved.

I was fully involved, yet trying to be objective. I guess maybe my passion got the better of me. Some parents probably thought I was biased.

We're all biased.

We are. And I would tell the students, "This is my perspective and I want you to question me." That's why I always tried to bring in other people, but that only added more fuel to the flame. I brought in a member of the PLO. The guy is not anything flamboyant or anything—he's a computer programmer for Portland State, and he's an intellectual, and he's really a pacifist, and he doesn't belong to that party—well, the PLO was sworn off that at that time anyway, but that was just too much. So by my third year, I was put on another plan of assistance, only this time I could see the writing on the wall—they were trying to get rid of me. I just dug in and I enlisted as much support as I could. I had this woman whom I didn't know—but I knew she was a good evaluator—come in from Lewis and Clark. She evaluated me and wrote this incredible evaluation wishing that they would have teachers like me at Lewis and Clark. The administrators thought I had somehow manipulated that. Finally I said I wanted to take this to the school board. They kept me hanging. "If you just jump through this hoop." "If you just do this." So I did it all. Meanwhile, I was coming down with ovarian cancer and I didn't know it. I mean I had symptoms. I had pains. But I was so driven. Again, that drive in me, maybe the fundamentalist in me—you know, Daniel in the lion's den, persecution, you don't walk away with your tail between your legs. You fight. I really believed in my cause and that there was a growing sentiment against me because of my politics, but I couldn't put my finger on it. And it would be hard to fight that fight, so my attorney at the union said, "Well, we'll just prove that you're a good teacher and we'll get the community to speak up." Well, we packed the school house for two nights and it was the first time a teacher had had an open public meeting. Usually, they would accept the decision, they wouldn't want the publicity, but I wanted plain-out *open*. I was so sure I was going to win. I had students coming from college to speak out for me and I thought, *My God, I'm going to win this fight.* And then they said, well, they couldn't decide. It was too much to decide. They'd have to wait three weeks and let the administration put their case together. As though they hadn't had all year to put their case together. So we had to wait three more weeks and we packed the school house a second time, and it was midnight before they made their decision. And the decision was unanimously no, they would stand by the principal. I got a call later from one of the school-board members who had quit the school board that fall, and who apologized to me and said they knew they were doing the wrong thing, but it was like a Pandora's box. If they allowed me to challenge this and win, what precedents would be set?

That must have been very hard.

It was such a defeat, such an enormous defeat, because I identified myself as a teacher. I saw myself as a teacher. And within five days, my symptoms were really exaggerated. I could barely walk. I was ill. And in two weeks I was in the hospital, and within a month I was diagnosed with ovarian cancer.

Do you feel that those things were connected?

I did at the time. In fact, I went and saw a civil-rights attorney and I managed to file a stress claim. I wanted to have it be more than a stress claim. I felt like they had destroyed my life and my health. But I realized I couldn't put it all on them, because I also ignored the symptoms. I also was bullheaded and should have walked away. I should have gone straight to the hospital in May or April when I was feeling pain, but I was used to menstrual pain. I had endometriosis and I thought it was stress.

What sort of symptoms did you have?

I had achey pain in my back. That was really my only symptom. This ache. When I would get into the car after school and sit down in the car, it would press like where my kidneys are on each side, and it would kind of hurt—kind of a soft, sensual pain, not a stabbing pain—and I was thinking, *Oh, it must be just stress*. But then in the three weeks between the two school-board meetings, I had to buy a new dress—my dress size had enlarged. Everything else was the same but my belly—I developed ascites. And after the decision came out, I could hardly walk; the ascites was really bad, out to here. Fortunately, I had an infection going too, so I spiked a fever of 104 one night, which got me into the emergency room, and by the next day they had drawn off all this fluid. So for two weeks we didn't know what it was, but then I think it was September 7th—they did surgery and I was diagnosed with stage-III ovarian cancer. I think if I had acted earlier, it would at least have been stage-II which really increases your chances of survival. So I was very bitter. I did get an out-of-court settlement from them: $5,000. But that was in 1993. My life has been completely different since then. Before that time, my friend Dina and I had produced a documentary on Cambodian-refugee women, and that was a wonderful period when we became real close to a lot of people, and we got a Silver Reel award for it and did a really good job. We worked with a great engineer who did the sound design. I realized then I'm not just a teacher, but that I've always wanted to integrate radio into the classroom. Anytime I did a radio piece, I would bring it in. I found that radio was very effective. The kids weren't distracted by images. But they're also intolerant. "What, it's not a video?" But if I played little parts and turned off the lights and had them write stuff down and think about it, it was more of an intellectual thing. So after I got sick, I thought, *Well, this is it. I'll never teach again*. But I did manage to keep my certificate. I did do enough classes so I've got my certificate, should that day happen. And

I got drawn more into the Old Mole. We stuck with that. And we did short pieces on ordinary people. Our tapes have often been on women, like women in the labor movement, or like Elizabeth Linder: women activists, older women, immigrants, people marginalized, ordinary people with real extraordinary stories—giving those people a voice. I've taken those into the classroom and I've also helped organize workshops with the World Affairs Council on how to use radio in the classroom. We now sell our tapes to teachers and universities. Plus it's knitted me closely to various communities like anthropology would. You know, you don't have to do a documentary. But then I am the front person. I'm the pearl diver. I go out and get the pearls and bring them to Dina, and she helps me fit them all together into a beautiful necklace.

It's glorious having someone you work so well with.

It is. To have a partner, like I said—our chemistry and our friendship. She has been the most loyal friend imaginable. We just finished this last piece. We got funding for both documentaries from the Humanities Council. Dina does the grant writing and she's our business manager. But I do know how to get the stories and I do know how to cultivate the people, and then I end up with all these friends.

You're quite a communal sort of person, aren't you? Do you think that comes from your family situation?

We had a big extended family outside of our little family, and I think especially after my dad was hurt, before he got cancer, the whole family rallied. Plus we had a church family, and there was something communal about that. So there was always a sense that you didn't just live your life for yourself. You definitely shouldn't live your life for yourself. I mean that's terrible. You live your life for others and family. I've had to get over some of that. Christmas, my parents' idea of Christmas, is you bring in everybody who has nobody to keep Christmas with. Like the old country. You don't just spend it with your little family. Or

Thanksgiving. We've had to struggle with my mother around this. In recent years it's become more important for me to have time with just my family. When you feel your time may be limited, your priorities change. I guess getting cancer has been another turning point in my life. See this article? I hate that. I just hate that attitude, where this person says, "If I cry, I feel like the cancer's getting the best of me." You know, this is clearly a thirty-year-old woman who's been diagnosed, but has never had a recurrence and probably has had only one dose of chemotherapy, and she's beaten it. It's just the American power of positive thinking. The book that has affected me most profoundly in my cancer journey has been Susan Sontag's *Illness as Metaphor*, in which she says, basically, there's the kingdom of the well and the kingdom of the ill. She compares the way tuberculosis was treated in literature in the 19th century with the way cancer is treated in the 20th century, how they're overly metaphorized. Like, "crime is a cancer." To be a really great poet, TB was almost obligatory. Whereas, cancer! Both diseases nobody knew what caused them. A lot of anxiety comes with that. And so to fill that vacuum, people would make up all this stuff about them. We don't know what causes cancer. We can't control it. This idea that you can will the cancer away, can visualize it away. I mean, there may be an element of truth in that. But if you have a recurrence, then you have to deal with the guilt. It's cruel and it's wrong and it's facile. I've been struggling with cancer for three and a half years. I've had a bone-marrow transplant. I've had chemotherapy. I've had I-don't-know-how-many surgeries and how-many recurrences and I'm still alive. I feel and I know that hope is important in fighting cancer. You've got to keep your fighting spirit. You've got to stay hopeful, but I've also these last three and a half years been in psychoanalysis. Maybe not formal psychoanalysis, but psychotherapy with someone with a psychoanalytic perspective, and it's given me the ability to really explore this. And I think how sad for people going through an illness, if they're afraid to express anything negative for fear that negativity might fuel the illness.

Yet we know that repressed negativity can torture a person.

Of course it was a foreigner that brought that to our shores! I don't know if we would ever have come up with that ourselves. We tend to think everything is your own fault, you know, *your* poverty, *your* illness, it's *your* fault. Blame the victim. That's why I'm hesitant to say the stress caused my cancer. I don't know what caused it. I do know the stress distracted me and probably didn't help my immune system, but I do know that since the cancer I have been doing writing, trying to write about the cancer, and it also has become real important to me to someday produce a radio piece on women and ovarian cancer. After my bone-marrow transplant, I had well over a year of remission and good health and I was able to really get to work. We even went to Italy. In a sense, cancer has freed me to be myself in a way I wasn't before. I can be honest and I can say "I don't want to be with this person, I don't want to spend time this way." Before I would have been the good girl I'd grown up to be, put aside my personal feelings, and suffered, tolerated being around people I didn't want to be around, and now I don't. I really am much more of a so-called bitch. I mean in some ways. But I also have come to appreciate my family and friends who have supported me through this. You are always alone with your cancer, but you can't fight it alone.

But I don't feel any need to apologize like I used to. I don't worry about the same things I used to. I don't rehearse in my head what it was I said or should have said. I don't really care about those things.

Why?

It all seems like drops. When you're faced with death, profoundly faced with death, it does transform you in a major way.

What do you care about?

I care about life and I care about the same things I've always cared about. I care about my husband, Joe, who has been my anchor and best friend, and about my family and friends. I want to continue, I've wanted to continue to do the work, almost with a fevered passion, more fevered, but I also feel like I have a right to my own feelings. I have a right to my own path. Nobody can say anything to me now. I have cancer, and in a way, it's a freeing experience. You also come through feeling you are a lot stronger than you ever thought you were. I always knew I was strong, but I didn't know how strong. There is something in me—the will to live that I imagine most people have, but I've discovered that I have this grit. The grit that I discovered when I was fifteen years old. Even when I was a child, I had a certain identity about me. They called me Pepper Pot, you know? I remember I could be blunt and say what I wanted. I was allowed that in the family. I was the clown. I could make my mother laugh. When she was crying, I tried to make her laugh. Although my sister Jan is the only one who made me laugh. She taught me how to laugh. She was my biggest audience, my biggest fan. Jan. But then when I turned fifteen, it was like I couldn't be that anymore. I had to be an angel. I had to be an angel. I had to hold it together. I had to repress any hostility I might be feeling. But little by little, I've discovered my strength.

When I fought the school board—you know that song, "I fought the law and the law won?" Well, I felt like I was fighting for my job and for my integrity. When I lost, when they gave their verdict, it was my oldest sister, Linda, who stood up and launched into this thing, and I thought she'd go on and on and on. You see in our family, people will start praying and will go on and on, but she said, "Shame on you. Shame on all of you. Look what you've done. What have you modeled to these students here in letting go of this fine teacher? Shame on you."

And they all listened to her. You could have heard a pin drop. I have an incredible family. We really stand by each other. My brother Randy—he's a fisherman now—he looks just like his father; he has my father's hands, he'd do anything for me. And even my oldest brother. He's heartbroken that I may die in sin, die without repenting. He agonizes over that. These are not people that take souls lightly. He loses sleep over that. And I don't know, maybe in the end I will repent. I don't know. I can't predict because it's a terrifying thing and I want to leave it open. I don't want anybody to judge. All I know is that I will not go gently into the night.

Joan died at 3 A.M. on June 4th with her family by her side.

The Last Pages

"Voir Dire" had two sources. First, I was a juror for a somewhat similar murder trial in Boston several years ago. Second, a good friend of mine, Richard Haesler, is a public defender in Burlington, Vermont, and his work and his life—combined with the trial—seemed to provide a ready-made story. As it happens, I ended up cutting most of the references to my friend in the final draft, but still, I hope "Voir Dire" serves as a worthy tribute.

NOMI EVE

In memory.

Ishai Buch
1913-1948

Peretz Buch
1913-1991

This picture was taken on the last day of my good friend's life. Though you cannot tell from this picture, her body is riddled with tumors. Her name was Kessel and in this picture she is forever eight years old.

I have always been a dog person (as opposed to a non-dog person, or a cat person, etc.), and cannot recall a time in my life when I did not have a dog or at least live with someone who did. I suppose this is the reason why dogs so often crop up in my writing, though I can say with relief that I've never known a dog remotely resembling the mastiff in "The Breathable Air."

I do not know what inspired this story. Seeing the sunlight fall on my grandmother's hands? Having the decision to put Kessel to sleep resting on my shoulders, then holding her head in my lap during and in the moments after? Both these things, of course, and many others too, not the least of which is my marriage and my wonderful wife, Kathryn. It is to her and her sweet spirit that I dedicate this story.

Karen Outen

The biggest surprise in writing "What's Left Behind" was the emergence of Mose Job, who seemed initially to be a recurring cartoonish memory. When the story was finished, I found it difficult to leave him. I've written a good deal of autobiographically-based fiction, but this story was prompted by the term "flattened affect," which cropped up in a conversation with my cousin, who is a psychiatrist. Later, on an emotionally challenging day, I joked with a friend about feeling flattened by life. And then Maggie started to tell me her story.

My life and my family are not featured in this story, but I'd like to honor my family somehow (my eighty-five relatives provide a major source of writing inspiration). So, here's a picture of me and my sister Gwen, taken when I was ten and she was ten months. She's usually open to having a disguised appearance in my stories, but she was grateful to miss this tragic flood.

Ann Hood

My father has been battling lung cancer since last October. As I write this, he is lying in the hospital, struggling for every breath. My mother and I take turns staying with him, sleeping in reclining chairs in his room. These past months, my life has been very schizophrenic. My baby Grace was born one week before my father was diagnosed. A new baby, young children who don't understand what is happening around them, deadlines, the holidays, hope, and despair have been part of every day. What is getting me through this? Love. My parents were the most loving parents anyone could have as I was growing up; they also demonstrated daily the love between them. In junior high, I was embarrassed by their handholding in public. As an adult, I admire it. This is their wedding picture, November 11, 1950. For over forty-six years they have been a model of what a good marriage should be. Even today, that remains unchanged. They taught me courage, joy, love, and faith. I rely on those things daily.

Kevin Canty

This is a photograph that my wife, Lucy Capeheart, took at a swap meet in rural Florida. You can't quite feel the heat of the afternoon, but you can see the storm clouds rolling in off the Gulf. We lived in the South for four years without ever exactly feeling at home. It's the American Bad Place and the Soul Place, the land of chemical plants, pork barbecue, Muddy Waters, and rusty Cadillacs. The good parts and the bad parts are all mixed up together and it's hard to know what's at the heart of it.

We're back in Montana now, back where we mostly both know what's going on around us, but the South persists. Sometimes we both just want to be hot, want to sit around in the carport in shorts and a tank top, drinking gin and slapping mosquitoes, and listening to our friends tell stories. I wrote this story, "Little Debbie," out of the memory of Southern accents and out of the songs of Steve Earle, Vic Chesnutt, and Blind Willie Johnson, with thanks.

Past Contributing Authors and Artists

Issues 1 through 23 are available for eleven dollars each.

Robert H. Abel • Linsey Abrams • Steve Adams • Susan Alenick • Rosemary Altea • A. Manette Ansay • Margaret Atwood • Aida Baker • Brad Barkley • Kyle Ann Bates • Richard Bausch • Robert Bausch • Charles Baxter • Ann Beattie • Barbara Bechtold • Cathie Beck • Kristen Birchett • Melanie Bishop • Corinne Demas Bliss • Valerie Block • Harold Brodkey • Danit Brown • Kurt McGinnis Brown • Paul Brownfield • Judy Budnitz • Evan Burton • Gerard Byrne • Jack Cady • Annie Callan • Kevin Canty • Peter Carey • Carolyn Chute • George Clark • Dennis Clemmens • Evan S. Connell • Wendy Counsil • Toi Derricotte • Tiziana di Marina • Junot Díaz • Stephen Dixon • Michael Dorris • Siobhan Dowd • Barbara Eiswerth • Mary Ellis • James English • Tony Eprile • Louise Erdrich • Zoë Evamy • Nomi Eve • Edward Falco • Michael Frank • Pete Fromm • Daniel Gabriel • Ernest Gaines • Tess Gallagher • Louis Gallo • Kent Gardien • Ellen Gilchrist • Mary Gordon • Peter Gordon • Elizabeth Graver • Paul Griner • Elizabeth Logan Harris • Marina Harris • Erin Hart • Daniel Hayes • David Haynes • Ursula Hegi • Andee Hochman • Alice Hoffman • Jack Holland • Noy Holland • Lucy Honig • Linda Hornbuckle • David Huddle • Stewart David Ikeda • Lawson Fusao Inada • Elizabeth Inness-Brown • Andrea Jeyaveeran • Charles Johnson • Wayne Johnson • Thom Jones • Cyril Jones-Kellet • Elizabeth Judd • Jiri Kajanë • Hester Kaplan • Wayne Karlin • Thomas E. Kennedy • Jamaica Kincaid • Lily King • Maina wa Kinyatti • Jake Kreilkamp • Marilyn Krysl • Frances Kuffel • Anatoly Kurchatkin • Victoria Lancelotta • Doug Lawson • Jon Leon • Doris Lessing • Janice Levy • Christine Liotta • Rosina Lippi-Green • David Long • Salvatore Diego Lopez • William Luvaas • Jeff MacNelly • R. Kevin Maler • Lee Martin • Alice Mattison • Eileen McGuire • Gregory McNamee • Frank Michel • Alyce Miller • Katherine Min • Mary McGarry Morris • Bernard Mulligan • Abdelrahman Munif • Kent Nelson • Sigrid Nunez • Joyce Carol Oates • Tim O'Brien • Vana O'Brien • Mary O'Dell • Elizabeth Oness • Mary Overton • Peter Parsons • Annie Proulx • Jonathan Raban • George Rabasa • Paul Rawlins • Nancy Reisman • Linda Reynolds • Anne Rice • Roxana Robinson • Stan Rogal • Frank Ronan • Elizabeth Rosen • Janice Rosenberg • Kiran Kaur Saini • Libby Schmais • Natalie Schoen • Jim Schumock • Barbara Scot • Amy Selwyn • Bob Shacochis • Evelyn Sharenov • Ami Silber • Floyd Skloot • Gregory Spatz • Lara Stapleton • Barbara Stevens • William Styron • Liz Szabla • Paul Theroux • Abigail Thomas • Randolph Thomas • Joyce Thompson • Patrick Tierney • Andrew Toos • Patricia Traxler • Christine Turner • Kathleen Tyau • Michael Upchurch • Daniel Wallace • Ed Weyhing • Joan Wickersham • Lex Williford • Gary Wilson • Terry Wolverton • Monica Wood • Christopher Woods • Celia Wren • Brennan Wysong • Jane Zwinger

James Gipso Sayer, facing the camera in Seattle.

Coming next:

You can't go it alone. It's too hard, and it's unnecessary. It's true that in marriage you have to give a little. You have to close your eyes to certain things. But it's a cold world, and everybody needs a home fire. Marriage is worth the compromises. He has always said that, although not lately.

from "Solitaire" by Patricia Page

Sometimes I can better describe a person by another person's reaction. In a story in my first book, I couldn't think of a way to describe the charisma of a certain boy, so the narrator says, "I knew girls who saved his chewed gum."

from an interview with Amy Hempel
by Debra Levy and Carol Turner

Charlie was upset. He is at the stage where everything must be in order. He cannot tolerate a jacket whose zipper is not zipped up. He puts the tops back on his magic markers. He collects his pail and shovel from the sandbox before he gets out.

from "The Croup" by Gail Greiner